FOGTOWN

FOGTOWN

A NOVEL

Peter Plate

SEVEN STORIES PRESS

New York • London • Toronto • Melbourne

Seven Stories Press
140 Watts Street
New York, NY 10013
www.sevenstories.com

IN CANADA
Publishers Group Canada, 250A Carlton Street, Toronto, ON M5A 2L1

IN AUSTRALIA
Palgrave Macmillan, 627 Chapel Street, South Yarra VIC 3141

IN THE UK
Turnaround Distribution, Unit 3, Olympia Trading Estate,
Coburg Rd., Wood Green, London N22 6TZ

College professors may order examination copies of Seven Stories Press titles
for a free six-month trial period. To order, visit www.sevenstories.com/textbook/
or fax on school letterhead to 212.226.1411.

Cover design by Krista Vossen
Text design by India Amos

LIBRARY OF CONGRESS CATALOGING-IN-PUBLICATION DATA

Plate, Peter.
Fogtown : a novel / Peter Plate.—Seven Stories Press 1st ed.
p. cm.
ISBN 1-58322-639-7 (pbk. : alk. paper)
1. San Francisco (Calif.)—Fiction. 2. Inner cities—Fiction. I. Title.
PS3566.L267F64 2004
813'.54—dc22
2003027062

Printed in Canada
9 8 7 6 5 4 3 2 1

FOGTOWN

ONE

A T SUNRISE on the last day of summer an armored car exited the freeway near the police station and rumbled down Market Street toward the Embarcadero. Inscribed in blue letters on the transport's sides was the name of the company it belonged to: Brinks. In smaller red-inked lettering were the words: subsidiary of Pittston.

Fog was murdering the street. Blotting it out with a greasy haze that was no higher than a foot off the ground. The fashion boutiques and chi-chi restaurants that lined the avenue were ghostly white in the mist. The imported trees planted in front of the tourist hotels were forlorn and wet. The beggars, pickpockets, hookers, and bicycle thieves who habitually worked the sidewalks from dawn until twilight were no place in sight.

While waiting for the Social Security office to open, Mama Celeste watched the Brinks truck pass the Warfield Theater. A San Francisco Giants baseball hat sat on top of her dreadlocks; a faded knee-length purple smock hung from her thin, stooped frame. Dead leaves swirled around her feet and flirted with her orthopedic shoes. Her favorite Vietnam-era green army jungle jacket wasn't doing much to ward off the morning's chill.

Mama's high-yellow face was a billboard of disappointment. It was the third week of the month and she hadn't received her retirement check yet. The check was supposed to be in the mail. Maybe someone had stolen it. Or maybe it had gotten lost. It was all a mystery. What the post office did. What the government did.

She threw a wry glance at the other retirees in the Social Security line. There must have been eighty people. Old men and women dressed in winter clothes because the San Franciscan summer was cold enough to freeze the marrow in your bones. The queue snaked past the boarded-up Saint Francis Theater, an abandoned movie-house that was being torn down for condominiums, and went around the corner onto Sixth Street. "What a bunch of fools we are," Mama muttered.

The night before, Mama Celeste had been visited in her sleep by a demon. She had been in bed shortly after midnight. A foghorn was sounding near Point Bonita in the bay. She opened one eye and there was the demon, naked with wings on his back. His eyebrows were shaved. His hairline had a widow's peak. His flinty orbs gleamed with a luminosity that made Mama think his presence was a prelude to death. Her death. She coughed and smelled brimstone. She was terrified. She wasn't ready for the afterlife. She had things to do here on earth.

The demon passed wind, a viscous green-tinted cloud that scorched the wallpaper. He leaned over her, his chin chaffing her teats. "You virago," he harped, "why are you so stubborn? You have to come with me. It's time."

Willing herself to be strong, Mama replied, "I ain't going anywhere."

The dybbuk had laughed uproariously at her defiance and then vanished.

Mama continued to stare at the Brinks lorry as it inched by the Social Security office. The taillights bled into the fogginess. Oversized tires swished against the damp asphalt. A line of smoke hissed from the exhaust pipe.

Out of nowhere, a Ford Taurus sedan careened onto Market Street. The car drunkenly crossed the yellow dividing line in the road. Instead of doubling back, the Taurus sliced in front of the Brinks truck and clipped the front bumper. Recoiling from the impact, the sedan boomeranged onto the sidewalk, crashing into a fire hydrant.

The Brinks vehicle fared no better. The driver lost control of the steering wheel and bumped his head against the bulletproof windshield, knocking himself unconscious. The truck went up on two wheels and rolled over on its side with tires spinning, raising red and white sparks, and mashing a telephone pole. The pole caved into a Payless Shoe Store window. A salvo of glass shards ripped into the store's awnings.

The guard watching the money in the back was thrown to the floor. The armor-plated rear door cracked open and piles of cash somersaulted onto the macadam. Stacks of brand new one-hundred-dollar bills destined for a bank scattered over the roadbed, blending in with cigarette butts, beer cans, used condoms, and cigar wrappers.

Bills lay in heaps on the pavement. Pushed by the breeze, money clogged the doorways of Bora's Café and the House of Blue Jeans. Dunes of Andrew Jacksons rested on sewer grates. One-hundred-dollar bills decorated the sidewalk, along with used syringes, empty crack bags, and McDonald's hamburger cartons. A column of black smoke rose from under the Brinks truck's hood. One of its giant wheels kept turning.

Being a religious woman, Mama Celeste was convinced she was having a vision. The money had to be an omen. It was a sign from God, a message from Him to everyone. Judgment day had finally come.

From three blocks away, police sirens keened.

The cash and the pensioners were gone by the time the cops arrived at the scene of the accident.

By eight in the morning the police were frantic to find the Brinks money. The first reports of its whereabouts were not encouraging. No witnesses had come forward. Both Brinks personnel had been hospitalized. The driver was in the intensive care unit at St. Mary's Medical Center on Hayes Street and was unable to talk. The guard was in a coma in the trauma unit. The guys in the Ford Taurus had evaporated, leaving behind their car, which turned out to be stolen from a repair garage in Daly City.

Market Street cuts the city in half, running east from Twin Peaks down to the San Francisco Bay shoreline. From Twin Peaks you can see Mount Diablo thirty miles away in the East Bay, the blue and brown Sonoma hills to the north, and the Farallon Islands in the Pacific Ocean. A typical day on Market Street has at least one shooting, or if nothing else, a stabbing and an armed robbery.

The Allen Hotel sat in the middle of Market Street halfway between the Castro district and the Tenderloin. A hundred-year-old flophouse that had fallen upon less than prosperous times, the brick hotel was five stories tall. The security gate was useless, hanging from one hinge. The windows that dimpled its facade were fusty. An unemployed flagpole protruded from the tarpaper roof. Dance studios, art supply stores, cafés, and nouveau cuisine restaurants—new businesses that were central to the chamber of commerce's drive to revitalize and spruce up the neighborhood—surrounded the boarding house and took the shine out of it.

A widow with no children, Mama Celeste had dwelled on the Allen's top floor for seven years. Her room was furnished with an iron-frame queen-size bed, two folding chairs, a table, an oak chest, a woven straw rug, and a dozen watercolor paintings on the walls.

Mama was aggravated. Rummaging through the chest's drawers, her salt-and-pepper eyebrows were knitted in a single line. Her iron-gray dreadlocks were pulled back from her lined, tallowy forehead with a thick red rubber band. Her printed frock, a twenty-year-old gift from her late husband, was shapeless from frequent laundering. Being half Jewish and half Puerto Rican, the rich color of Mama's skin and her regal nose had been inherited from her father. Her bad feet and kinky hair came from her mother's side of the family. They were from Warsaw in Poland.

Nearly eighty years of age, Mama was forgetful. Her memory waxed and waned. She had good days when she remembered every small thing. She had bad days when the lights in her head were switched off. She misplaced items, and she was unable to remember where she'd put things.

For a split second, Mama didn't know where she was. She didn't hear the traffic on Market Street. She didn't hear her neighbors fighting next door. She didn't hear the mice scrambling under the floor. She didn't hear the clock tick-tocking on the nightstand. She didn't smell the mold in her room. She didn't see the cockroaches skitter across the carpet. She didn't feel the lumbago in her back. She felt and saw nothing. Then sensed what she'd been searching for, a Safeway supermarket shopping bag tucked underneath a tablecloth in the chest's bottom drawer, and she snapped back to reality.

The bag was coated with grease spots and had a tear down one side. She pried it from the drawer and lugged it across the room and tossed it on the bed. The bedsprings squealed in irritation as she plopped down on the mattress beside the bag.

Light-headed, she went blank for a moment. Her heart pounded. Was she getting a stroke? Maybe she was catching a cold. That would lead to pleurisy, and then she'd end up in the hospital. Since she was alone, no family or anyone, who would come to her rescue? She didn't want to think about it.

Mama had ended up at the Allen for the reasons most people washed up at a residential hotel—she had little money. A room didn't cost much. It gave you the space to contemplate your life. It was also someplace to get injured in. If the weather wasn't warm, your room was an icebox. The mold in the walls got in your lungs. You contracted asthma. The last stop was pneumonia.

Pneumonia's earmarks were an orchestra. You were hot and cold at the same time. You were hypersensitive to the touch. Because you had a blistering fever, a trip to the bathroom was no less arduous than rappelling up a mountainside. The disease preyed on the isolated and sought out the weak. If you were old, it was a murderer.

Fishing in the bag, she extracted a bleached muslin cloth sack emblazoned with bloodstains. The thing was heavy and she grimaced

5

with the effort it took to get it out. Printed in bold blue letters on the sack was the inscription: Property of Brinks.

She opened it and turned it upside down. A stack of crisp one-hundred-dollar bills fell in her lap and onto the blankets. A dozen other Ben Franklins frolicked to the rug in a lazy poetic trail. Mama Celeste laughed as she stooped over to retrieve them. The money was manna from heaven.

A yell in the hall interrupted her. Holding her breath, Mama was afraid. She listened carefully to every sound in the room. The faucet in the sink was dripping. The floorboards were creaking. The light bulb on the ceiling sizzled. Monstrous green flies buzzed at the window.

She couldn't recall a day when she hadn't been scared. Fear was in her blood. But it was odd how rapidly things changed. Two hours ago she'd been at the Social Security office on Market Street without a dime in her pocket. Then a miracle had occurred—God had communicated with her. He had done it for a reason.

Mama closed her eyes and replayed the Brinks crash. Money had poured out of the vehicle, more cash than she'd ever seen before. The guard inside the truck had been deathly pale; his khaki uniform was drenched with blood. Mama Celeste had felt bad for him, but when she saw the Franklins stacked ankle-deep on the pavement, she felt even worse for herself. Being hungry all the time could do that to a person. So could being penny-poor. It made you selfish.

Crossing the street, she went to the truck's door. Taking a Kleenex, she'd dabbed at the gash in the guard's forehead to staunch his wound. But seeing that it didn't do him any good, she clawed a sack of cash out from under his boots. That put her in a trance. The money had her head swimming. The other pensioners flitted over to the truck from the Social Security office. Moving fast, Mama stashed the bag under her coat. While everybody else was busy fighting over what cash there was on the ground, she beat a path homeward to the Allen Hotel.

Back in her room, Mama hid the legal tender in the chest and then fell on her knees to pray. She screwed her eyes shut, pressed her palms together, and asked God what she should do with the loot. Mama had been a non-unionized nurse's aide for most of her adult life. She'd toiled in hospices and rest homes. Having a ton of money was unfathomable. The question she posed to Him was on basic economics.

"Well, Lord," she incanted, "what do you want from me?"

God didn't waste any time getting back to her. He answered her prayers in a jiffy and instructed her what to do with the dough.

Mama gathered the money on the bed and then loaded it into an empty Reebok shoebox. Placing Ben Franklins in the box, she lost count of how much was in it after two hundred thousand dollars. Big numbers made her dizzy.

After filling up the shoebox to the brim, she threw the remaining cash back in the muslin Brinks sack. Dropping the sack in the Safeway shopping bag, Mama heaved herself off the bed. Her feet hurt like the dickens. So did her knees. She had worked hard for forty years, and this was what had happened. Her body was an assortment of pains and sometimes she hated it. The bag in hand, she slogged over to the oak chest and returned the booty to its hideout.

She made a cup of chamomile tea on the hot plate and then sat in a chair by the window and drank it, watching the butterflies cavort outside. The fog had lifted; the sun was getting higher, reaching over the rooftops. She rinsed the cup, put it on the counter next to the sink, set the shoebox by the door, and donned her army coat. As she did that, she had a glimpse in the mirror. What she saw disappointed her.

Her *punim* was a road map of seven-plus decades. Her nose was too large for the rest of her face. Her eyes were close-set and made her seem angry even when she was happy. The grooves in her mouth never expressed joy. Her chin was sharp as an axe. The furrows on her forehead were deep enough to plant corn in. No wonder she had no one to keep her company nowadays. With a *punim* like hers, who would want to?

She buttoned the coat to the collar, tied a yellow cotton handkerchief around her dreads, and crowned the ensemble with her Giants baseball hat. Safety-pinning her house keys to the coat's inner sleeve,

Mama Celeste picked up the shoebox, shuffled to the door, and opened it.

The melody of Oliver Nelson's jazz standard "Stolen Moments" greeted her in the dusty hallway. A neighbor had the tune on upstairs. A baby's high-pitched weeping wafted in from the airshaft. A man was singing while taking a shower in the communal bathroom. Mama Celeste shut her rickety door and keyed the deadbolt.

Certain the shoebox was snug in her arms, she went down four dark flights of stairs. She stopped at the landing on the third floor to catch her breath. A calico cat nipped past her and went out the window and onto the fire escape. The feline's orange-flecked fur glinted in the sun that was getting through the fog.

The Allen Hotel's lobby was a postage stamp–sized rectangle of marble floor. The walls were spray-painted with graffiti. Uncollected bags of trash garrisoned the corners. Cobwebs choked the ceiling. Judging by the number of them on the floor, letters to hotel occupants from the probation department at the Hall of Justice were the most popular kind of mail.

Enthroned on a milk crate in the foyer was the building's manager, a stocky, middle-aged ex-con named Jeeter Roche. Attired in a chartreuse polyester leisure suit and tan buck loafers, and smoking a hand-rolled Bugler cigarette, Jeeter was reading a paperback novel by Tadeusz Konwicki, the dissident Polish writer from the 1970s.

He pored over a sentence, taking pleasure in the author's writing style. The lobby's dim light burnished Jeeter's shaved pate. Tobacco smoke bedeviled his pointed ears. The paperback's pages were annotated with ballpoint pen markings, scoring his favorite passages. Books were Jeeter's obsession. His jacket pockets always bulged with a tatty paperback or two. The hotel lobby, along with everything else at the Allen, was his private kingdom. Every week Jeeter collected one hundred and seventy dollars in rent from each of the hotel's eighty tenants. A hundred and sixty was for the owner; the other ten was for Jeeter.

In addition to the fee he charged the tenants, Jeeter had another enterprise at the Allen. The owners, the city's premier slumlords, in exchange for his managerial services, had given him and his wife Chiclet a rent-free room on the second floor. Jeeter was using it and the rest of the hotel to sell a variety of drugs. He had some joints in his shirt pocket, one-papered reefers sprinkled with Peruvian coke flakes. Nobody in the building wanted them, so he'd smoked one for breakfast. The buzz had his head in a vise grip. Made his teeth ache from grinding them.

Selling dope was tolerable. The cash flow was consistent and it gave him extra hours to indulge in books that he ordinarily wouldn't have chanced. Lately he'd been reading William Shirer's *The Rise and Fall of the Third Reich*. It was slow going; the print required a magnifying glass.

Reading was a survival skill that Jeeter had acquired in prison. He'd been languishing in county jail, waiting for a transfer to the penitentiary upstate, and came upon a dog-eared copy of a John Dos Passos trilogy in his cell. The book took weeks to read and had kept him from going insane with boredom.

Jeeter closed his paperback when he heard steps on the staircase. The movement meant only one thing: a tenant was approaching. He looked up to find Mama Celeste holding onto the railing as she made her way downstairs. Jeeter noted she was dressed for winter on a summer morning. He put the novel in his jacket, rubbed his eyes, and smiled. Jeeter had several types of smiles. There was the smile he'd learned while doing his first jolt for larceny. That was his everyday servile smile. Then there was the smile that he'd earned during a three-year bit for burglary. That was his serene smile. And there was his vocational smile. He employed the latter on Mama Celeste, snarking, "Hey, girl. Top of the morning to you."

Mama Celeste said an epithet under her breath. The landlord was speaking to her. He was a putrid man, worse than a Cossack. She was instantaneously defensive. "What do you want?"

Jeeter had a pull off his fag and said, "The rent. It's due today. That's why I'm sitting down here in the lobby, to let you and everybody else in the building know it." He winked at Mama Celeste. "You look ready for a snowstorm. Don't you get hot wearing that army jacket all the time?"

Mama turned beet-red. She was indignant. Jeeter Roche was a bully. Sitting on the milk crate with his flabby legs, the goniff reminded her of the demon in her dreams. "I get cold," she said flatly.

"You do? Well, turn up the heat in your room."

"There ain't any."

"What?"

"It doesn't work."

Jeeter had turned off the heat in the building to save money. The owners had asked him to do it, saying they'd split the profit with him. For Mama Celeste's benefit, Jeeter made out like he didn't know anything. "Oh, yeah?"

Mama wasn't buying his innocence. Her nostrils quivered in accusation. "You knew there was no damn heat."

The cigarette's smoke hid the dismay on Jeeter's rubbery face. She'd slipped that one in real nice. Essentially calling him a liar. Jeeter had stolen cars in his ill-starred career as a villain. He'd also robbed banks, not very successfully, and had thieved from department stores. But when all was said and done, that was in the distant past and he now considered himself an honest man. Miffed, he said, "Well, hell."

"I see what goes on around here. I ain't blind."

"Oh, yeah?" Jeeter retorted. "And what is it that you see?"

Mama showed her claws. "You and them drugs."

Jeeter switched off his vocational smile and resorted to his penal smile. It was a submissive smile, how a feral dog is submissive. You turn your back on the cur, and it goes for your throat. Jeeter's lips were veal-colored. His teeth were sharp and yellow. His tongue flicked sideways when he said, "Whatever I'm doing, that ain't your business, you hear?"

Unconsciously, Jeeter fingered his face. His livid skin was a mine-field of razor bumps and ingrown hairs. Shaving was daily purgatory, a personal holocaust. Choreographing his mouth, he coaxed a final drag from the roll-up. He exhaled, spat out flecks of tobacco, then flung the butt on the ground and crushed it under his loafers. His bulky muscles twitched under the leisure suit's antiquated polyester. He said without emotion, "You keep talking like you've been doing, Mama, and you and me, we're gonna have a disagreement. One that will be thorny." He added, "Have you got your money for me?"

Mama was hard of hearing when the subject wasn't to her liking. "What, the rent?"

Jeeter whipped out an embossed leather bound receipt book from another pocket in his jacket. The receipt book was his pride and joy; it spoke the language of his soul. He opened the book, licked his thumb, turned several pages, and smiled again, this time with warmth. "It says here in my ledger, you haven't given me no money yet for this week. You either pay up or I'm going to have to evict you. You know I don't want to do that. But it's the law."

Mama was aghast. "You'd evict me?"

"I'd have to." Jeeter was impassive. "The owners would make me."

An eviction in a city with a 1 percent vacancy rate in rental housing was a nightmare. It was a death warrant for a geriatric on a fixed income. Too agitated to respond to Jeeter Roche's threat, Mama Celeste moved stiffly past him and went out the yawning security gate.

It took Mama a few seconds to get used to the street. A trolley car rumbled past a row of stunted palm trees. Three homeless men saddled with sleeping bags sat on the pavement by the Allen Hotel. A pigeon winged overhead, arcing into the haze. The wind mischievously lifted the hem of her coat. She felt chilliness under her collar, but the money in the shoebox, about two hundred thousand dollars, lifted her spirits as she ambled to the corner of Gough Street.

TWO

A T NINE O'CLOCK THAT MORNING it began to rain. Lightning buzzed over the Golden Gate Bridge and Alcatraz Island. The city's piebald hills were shrouded in eggshell-colored clouds. The shower lambasted Market Street with deafening intensity, rebounding off the pavement like buckshot. Tourists held newspapers over their heads and ducked into doorways for cover.

The shift in the weather didn't stop the police response to the Brinks robbery. Teams of plainclothes agents from the department's intelligence unit fanned out in the Tenderloin to hunt for eyewitnesses. A squad of uniformed police officers, acting on an anonymous tip, searched the housing project for the aged on Polk Street. Radio and television news said a gang of well-organized thieves had pilfered over four million dollars.

The symphony of police car sirens on Market Street startled Stiv Wilkins, making him think he was back in jail. Rolling over in bed, he looked at his bride of ten months. She was snoring mouth open, dead to the world. Her shoulder-length bleached platinum blonde hair was splayed on the pillow. Matte black lipstick was daubed on her mouth. Her belly button was pierced with an eighteen-karat-gold ring. Her taut coppery breasts were swollen with milk. Their three-month-old baby boy was sleeping on her stomach.

Crawling out of the sack, Stiv padded over to the window to see what the brouhaha was about. Naked, he braced his hands on the sill. Pressing his aquiline nose to the cold glass, he gazed at the street. The rain was coming down in buckets. A string of black-and-white cop cars flashing red and blue lights were at the Bank of America building on Van Ness Avenue.

The Allen Hotel had been Stiv's residence for two years. Twenty-four months. Seven hundred and thirty days. Seventeen thousand five hundred and twenty hours. Ever since his band came to town on tour from Portland and fell apart. The drummer decided he was gay and left the group to join a drag queen revue, and the bass player went back to Oregon because the heroin was cheaper up north.

The room was ten feet wide and twelve feet long. The bed took up most of the floor. A sink was wedged in a corner and a Sony television was bolted to the wall. With three people in it, him, Sharona and the brat, the place was no better than a sardine can. Watching the cavalcade of police cars glide past the Allen Hotel toward Octavia Street and the cross-town freeway overpass, Stiv was anxious and tugged at the hair on his narrow chest.

The day before he'd had a beef with a dope dealer. It began when Richard Rood came up to him in the Orbit Café on Market Street. Stiv had been sitting alone at a table drinking a cup of black coffee and minding his own business. Richard was decked out in a gaudy red patent leather suit with a large American flag sewn on the back. His jacket was skintight, advertising his muscular chest. The pants rode high up the cleft in his ass, causing intense discomfort. Three zircon earrings gleamed in each ear. His ebony countenance profiled an oft-broken nose, chiseled cheeks, and deep-set brooding eyes.

A respiratory virus had been circulating throughout the Tenderloin. There was a dull tone to Richard Rood's skin, courtesy of the flu. Without being asked, he sat down at Stiv's table and issued bad vibes. He said, "Where in damnation have you been?"

Stiv was concise. "Around."

"We've got trouble."

"Who does?"

"You and me."

"We do?"

"For reals and I'm only going say four things here, dig? Let me chop it up for you," Richard said. "You've been fucking me. You can't turn shit into sugar and I don't want any excuses from you. I just want my money."

Stiv sipped at his coffee and remained poker-faced. He was resplendent in a red Pendleton shirt that he'd gotten at the flea market in Berkeley, blue Ben Davis jeans, and a black leather motorcycle jacket; his hair had been recently barbered into a modified quiff and was stiff with Brylcreem. His steel-toed Chippewa engineer boots were planted flat on the floor.

Richard's accusation was indisputable. The dealer had fronted Stiv an ounce of *mota* to sell. Not the good stuff, not Humboldt green; Richard didn't trust him with top-quality merchandise. The product had been Sinaloa dirt weed, a lousy grade that attacked your lungs as if it were napalm. The wholesale price to Stiv had been four hundred dollars. A tad inflated, but reasonable. Anything Stiv earned over that sum was his to keep. But Stiv wasn't a good businessman. Nor was he practical. Instead of selling the pot, he'd smoked the whole bag. Stiv knew he'd erred. It was no secret. And he didn't have the money. He didn't have anything. He had nada. He paused before answering Richard, taking his time, and then said, "I'm sorry, man. I ain't got it."

With a moue of disbelief, Richard Rood rolled his eyes and chastised him. "What did you do with the weed? Did you even sell it?"

Stiv demurred. "I didn't do a damn thing with it."

"Then where is it?"

"It's gone."

Richard zeroed in for the kill. "You smoked it, didn't you?"

"Did not."

"Did too. You've got it written all over your tired-ass face. You smoked it."

Stiv put the coffee cup on the table and threw his hands in the air. The gesture was saturated with defeat. "Okay, okay, I did. What can I say, dude? It's a weird time. I've got a wife and kid. I'm stressing and shit."

Because he was sick, Richard Rood's throat hurt and it was difficult to talk. He should've been at home in bed. Instead he was running all over town collecting his money. His nose was stuffed up and he couldn't inhale through his nostrils. His eyes flamed red with disgust as he said, "Once you dipped into the bag, you couldn't stop smoking. So you just kept going."

Rood's reputation had its origin in the puckered, cross-shaped blob of scar tissue that ornamented his forehead. Legend had it, a rival drug dealer dusted on PCP—the man believed he was the reincarnation of Judas Iscariot—had been mad at Richard for stealing a jar of morphine tablets. The rumor of the theft had spread in the ghetto with the speed of a venereal disease. Everyone knew a showdown was coming and that it would be nasty.

Exhibiting his customary disdain for no-count idiots, Richard had ignored the gossip and gone about his business. His mistake proved near fatal as his adversary cornered him in an alley one fine evening and shot him point-blank in the face with a .22 Colt derringer.

A derringer is a modest gun, suitable for low-key situations such as a brawl at a party or a rumble in a nightclub. For assassinations, it isn't adequate. The derringer's bullet, the kind of ordnance that was sold under the counter at swap meets, blossomed out of the barrel and hit Richard Rood in the head. But it failed to penetrate his skull. The slug planted itself between his eyebrows, sticking out of his skin like avant-garde jewelry.

Realizing he wasn't dead, Richard underwent a severe mood swing. Not having any family, he felt alone. More alone than he'd ever been in his life. That had hurt more than the bullet. Being vain, he was enraged that his flawless complexion had been marred. He tugged at the slug with his fingers, but couldn't get it out. Half-blinded from the blood running down his skin, he caressed the twisted piece of lead that was supposed to have killed him.

His foe took off, never looking back.

Because he was uneducated—a tenth-grade dropout from San Francisco's Galileo High School—Richard wasn't quite sure what the bullet in his noggin was supposed to mean. But from then on, his rep was sterling. No one ever dared to tangle with him.

Aware of Richard Rood's history, Stiv did an inventory on himself. He was young and didn't have a pot to piss in. The only thing he had going was a penchant for recklessness that bordered on self-destruction.

"Stiv, pay attention to me."

"Uh, what?"

"You don't know shit from Shinola. You are lower than a broke-dick dog."

Stiv's reply was marinated in resignation. "You're right."

Richard's jheri curls were a black corona around his face. He flexed his biceps and heard the distinct sound of a jacket inseam giving way. The cheap stitching in his suit was busting apart. "Sure as hell," he said. "You'll have to pony up that money."

Stiv parried. "And if I don't?"

"Further trouble will befall your ass."

The two men were sitting face-to-face. Except that the top of Richard's head was level with Stiv's chin. All sounds in the space between them died away, building disquietude polluted with cynicism. The other customers in the café had prudently departed. The counter-person was busy washing dishes in the back. Stiv was of two minds. Part of him said to drop it and walk away. Deal with the problem later. Worry about the money some other time. That was the passive Stiv. Another side of him wanted to get mad and cause a scene. That was his aggressive streak talking. But he was afraid of Richard. Crossing the man would earn him a one-way excursion to the morgue with a death certificate tied to his foot and a burial in a pine box. Thinking rapidly, he pontificated, "All right, man, I've got a plan."

Richard Rood wasn't impressed. "What is it?"

Stiv leaned forward and gave the dealer his most sincere look. The illumination in the café reflected the nervous warmth in his eyes. "Give me another day."

"To do what?"

"To get the money."

Rood smiled with heartfelt malevolence. His big white incisors were wet with spit. "And what if you don't come up with it?"

Stiv didn't know what was worse, the diminutive Richard, or his own rash mouthing. "Don't sweat it," he said confidently. "I'll get the cash."

Staring out the window at the rain, Stiv had other issues on his mind that were even worse than Richard Rood. The rent on the room at the Allen was overdue and the bookworm Jeeter Roche never took no for an answer. He was the type of building manager who never cut you any slack. If you didn't have the money, you were out on your ear.

Stiv had also gotten involved with Jeeter's wife. That had been another one of his quick-witted moves. The affair with her had been going up and down for weeks, and he was dying to end it. To cap it off he'd been seeing a ghost in the Allen Hotel.

The spook wore a pair of leather chaps studded with silver bells and a coarse white linen shirt. His feet were shod in rough cowhide boots. His youthful handsome face was haggard from exhaustion; his long black hair was matted in clumps. On the brocaded sash binding his waist were a holstered single-shot pistol and a sheathed butcher's knife. A braided quirt hung from his left wrist. His clothes were covered with the reddish-brown dust indigenous to the shores of the San Francisco Bay. His name was José Reyna. From Sonora in Mexico, he'd been an outlaw in the 1830s. San Francisco had been a sleepy bayside village populated with Mexicans, Ohlone and Miwok Indians, and gringo gold miners.

Stiv thought he was going bonkers and went to the mental health clinic on Shotwell Street. He was processed by a zealous twenty-seven-year-old psychiatric social worker out of UC Berkeley, a cat by the name of Norbert Deflass. Uniformed in a buttoned-down oxford shirt, pressed khakis, and topsiders with a cowlick in his hairdo, Deflass was courteous and enthusiastic, more like a shoe salesman than a social worker.

He ran Stiv through a battery of tests and then interviewed him, just the two of them in a whitewashed cubicle at the rear of the clinic. The room had two chairs and a desk. Norbert parked himself behind the desk, put his shoes on it, and said, "Look, Stiv, you're under a lot of pressure with having a kid and everything. How's your wife doing? How is she handling it?"

Stiv hunkered in a folding chair. He didn't like the look in Norbert's eyes. It was too friendly. "A lot better than me. She's a tough cookie."

"How old is she?"

"Nineteen."

"Wow, a baby mama. That's young. She must be a together kind of woman."

"Yeah, you could say that."

"Is your relationship stable?"

Stiv bristled. He didn't appreciate the question. His sex life wasn't the social worker's business. "What do you mean?"

"You're not planning on leaving her, are you, because of the kid?"

Stiv mulled it over. He decided not to say anything about the affair he was having. That was a separate issue. "No. I'm sticking it out. Like, family is important, you know?"

Deflass seemed to buy it. "Good, but here's the deal. I'm going to advise medication. You need something to smooth out the edges."

Stiv was nonplussed. "What's wrong with me?"

"I'm not a shrink, but I think you're borderline."

The diagnosis didn't mean a thing to Stiv. It was a jumble of words that he'd need a thesaurus to sort out. He was more curious about the drugs. They were more his style. He said, "What can you do for me?"

"I'm writing up a report for your doctor. I want him to give you a prescription to suppress the delusions. And Stiv?"

"What?"

"When you see things, when you have these episodes, do you hear voices?"

"Voices?"

"Yeah, people talking."

Stiv mused, "No, I see pictures. In technicolor."

"That's a hallucination."

"Yeah?"

"Yes. It's not a ghost. It's something internal that you're creating. Do you even know who José Reyna was?"

Stiv bobbed his chin in negation. "Nah, not before this."

"Allow me to explain it. You want to know?"

"Okay."

"Ever hear of these psychiatrists from England, R. D. Laing and Peter Cooper?"

"Nope."

"How about Gilles Deleuze and Felix Guattari?"

"Nah."

"They were like pioneers in their field. They'd say the hallucinations weren't a problem."

"Really?"

"You bet. It's how your subconscious is trying to heal itself."

This was mildly interesting to Stiv. "How's that?"

"By coming up with history. The truth is, you're experiencing a period of mental instability."

It was the last thing Stiv needed to hear. "What are you going to give me for this, uh, mental stuff."

"Haldol. You'll love it."

As the rain battered the window, Stiv became fearful. He hadn't talked to Norbert Deflass since yesterday. At the social worker's request his shrink gave him a script for Haldol, but the stuff hadn't been so wonderful. The drug plagued him with muscle spasms and cottonmouth. His brain was reduced to glue. Haldol benumbed his arms and legs and killed all feelings in his hands and feet. He stopped taking it after a day.

The baby was fussing in the bed and distracted Stiv. He turned around to see what was up. Straining to get at his mother's tits, the brat was tremulous, as though he had Parkinson's disease. His mouth was open; the glaze in his eyes was rabid. Sharona unbuttoned her black satin nightgown and whispered, "There, now, it's okay, Booboo."

Unhooking her nursing bra, she poked a breast in the infant's tyrannical mouth and he began to suck, gurgling heartily. Sharona half-closed her eyes and let the baby go to work, feeling the rhythm of her milk draining down his throat. She patted his fanny, and he dug his fingers in her hair, drooling on her gown. Finished with her tit, he chortled once and fell asleep.

Stiv walked over to the bed and sat down next to his son and wife. Sharona regarded him and the baby. The father of her child was a recent graduate of a six-month stint in county jail for selling nickel bags. Stiv often seemed no older than the infant. He had the same mindless expression on his face. It was a disconcerting comparison exacerbated by the fact that Stiv hadn't had a job in seven months. There was no food in the icebox. No money in the bank. She said to him, "You all right?"

He didn't answer her. How was he supposed to know if he was okay? His mind was a sieve, a Pandora's box. You opened it and ghosts came out. He got up and wandered to the closet, selected a pair of black Dickies, and stepped into them. He then went to the table and flipped on the radio. While absentmindedly listening to a news reporter talk about the Brinks truck robbery, Stiv concocted a scheme to get some cash. That was the number-one order of the day: improve his finances and pay the rent.

The radio newscaster was interviewing the chief of police about the Brinks caper. The chief's voice was impassioned with anger as he made a plea for the public to get involved. He said the robbers were criminals of the worst kind. Before the policeman went off the air, he gave out a snitch number for citizens to call if they had any information. Stiv fiddled with the radio dial and changed it to a jazz station, KCSM in San Mateo. Horace Silver's "Tokyo Blues" flowered into the room.

Listening to the music, Stiv flashed on Friedrich Nietzsche, the German philosopher. He liked fiction, Turgenev and Gogol, novelists whom his grandmother had advocated, but whenever Stiv was feeling blue, reading Nietzsche cheered him up. A quote came to mind: "Find an exalted and noble *raison d'être* in life; seek out destruction for its own sake."

Getting the rent together was going to be a bitch. The last time Stiv had gone out looking for money, he'd attempted to rob a mom-and-pop store in the Mission, a hole in the wall at Nineteenth and Lexington. It was an easy target. Nothing fancy. The place was empty. The street outside was quiet. It was a cakewalk. All he had to do was stick a gun in the proprietor's face and demand the loot. He'd done it before. He could do it in his sleep.

The minute he walked in the door, it went wrong. The Asian shopkeeper decided he didn't care for Stiv's looks, the black leather jacket and the chains, the sunglasses, or the rust-eaten revolver in his hand, and shot him with a chrome-plated .40 Smith and Wesson semiautomatic. The only reason Stiv was still alive was that the bullet struck the pocket watch he wore on his belt, stopping the hands at quarter of two.

Stiv shut the radio and went over to the sink, turned on the cold-water tap, and washed his face. He had to come up with five hundred and seventy bucks by the end of the day. Four hundred dollars was for Richard Rood. One hundred and seventy was for Jeeter Roche. Drying his neck with a threadbare towel, Stiv laughed. If he didn't get the money, he was as good as killed. Richard Rood would make sure of it.

THREE

THE RAIN STOPPED, as sudden as a heart attack. The sun, playing peek-a-boo with the fog, came out from behind a bank of offshore clouds. A rainbow curved over the Tenderloin's rooftops and sunshine dappled the marquees of Market Street's porno palaces. Looking in the window of the Donut Star coffee shop at Seventh and Market, Mama Celeste thinned her lips in consternation—nobody was in there.

Every morning Mama went to the Donut Star for a cup of coffee with her associates. She called them that because they weren't exactly her friends; they were acquaintances of long-standing repute. It was nothing special, just retired folks drinking coffee and talking. Mama was saddened. She'd come to depend on these meetings.

Now that the rain had ceased, steam was rising from the pavement. Sea gulls wheeled over the buildings. A train in the Southern Pacific rail yards on Fourth and Townsend blew its whistle. Two transvestite hookers carrying umbrellas and dressed in matching silver lamé pants suits and stiletto heels teetered past the Donut Star. The Muni bus shelter across the street was jam-packed with winos; a murder of crows perched on the shelter's roof. Waterlogged pigeons dive-bombed the stoplights and the stores on Jones Street, including Saint Anthony Dining Room, a venerable soup kitchen owned by the Catholic Church.

Mama didn't know what to do. She didn't want to go inside and drink coffee by herself. It was too lonely. But standing in the street wasn't healthy. Somebody might come up from behind and bonk her on the head. Knock her out, maybe shank her and take what she had. She didn't weigh a hundred pounds soaking wet. If someone wanted to mug her, she couldn't stop it.

Hugging the shoebox, Mama Celeste nudged the door and limped in. The first things that greeted her were the smells of fresh instant coffee and sausages burning on the grill, and a canned Tony Bennett ballad playing on the cheap-ass sound system. The short-order cook hailed her from behind the counter. He was pint-sized and barrel-chested in a T-shirt that was four sizes too small; a cold cigarette was wedged in his mouth and a squared-off Afro flossed his ears. "Good morning, Mama Celeste," he said. "How's it hanging with you?"

The dining area was empty. The brightly laminated yellow and blue plastic tables and booths were damp; the floor had been recently mopped. The fish bowl windows facing Market Street were streaked with cleaning powder. Mama Celeste answered the smiling black man in the bloody white apron with a wave of her hand. "I'm cool. Where's everybody?"

The short-order cook picked up a spatula and dug the sausages off the griddle. Flipping them onto a plastic plate, he reached in a pail of uncooked French fries, pulled out a handful, and threw them on the grill. He said, "The damn police got everyone all scared. No one's been in yet."

"How come?"

He swung around and stared at Mama Celeste. His blueberry black face was creased with sweat. His purpled eyes were fixed with concern. He put one gnarled hand on the counter, stuck out his beer belly, and squawked around the cigarette in his mouth. "Shit, woman, what's wrong with you? You blind? Look over there."

He pointed the spatula at the window. Where Market Street intersected at McAllister and Jones, there was a delta of police vehicles.

Cops in riot gear with assault rifles and bandoliers of stun grenades were laying down yellow crowd-control ticker tape. "That Brinks robbery has the police in a fucking tizzy," he said. "You hear about it?" Mama Celeste forced her face to remain inscrutable. "I ain't heard a damn thing."

"That's good," the cook chuckled, "because here comes one of them cops right now."

Pushing open the door to the Donut Star, patrolman Mandelstam made out his face in the glass. Cigarette ash was caked on the bib of his midnight blue combat tunic. His eyes were molten from sleeplessness. His fleshy cheeks were festooned with salt-and-pepper stubble. His nose was larger than a continent. Pausing in the doorway, he unstrapped his scuffed white riot helmet. The fluorescent lights in the coffee shop were too bright, too disorienting. He noted the dining area, and then the short-order cook. The black man looked back at the cop with no visible expression on his battered face. He simply nodded at Mandelstam and moved the cigarette in his mouth from left to right.

The silence in the place didn't feel right. Mandelstam couldn't put his finger on it, but something was off. The music was overly loud, like it was covering up something. Even the food cooking in the back smelled weird. Mandelstam sized up Mama Celeste at the counter. Maybe it was the crazy looking old lady. She couldn't have been more than four feet tall, not even with the mountain of dreadlocks on her head.

Retirees all looked alike to Mandelstam. He saw a million of them every day in the Tenderloin. Sitting in wheelchairs under liquor store awnings. Digging in trash bins for bottles to recycle. Feeding pigeons. Getting helped into ambulances. Standing in line at the welfare office. The old coot had her army coat zipped up to the collar, a stinky woolen muffler around her neck. The bill on her baseball hat was bent, covering her eyes. She had a decade-old Reebok shoebox in her hands.

If Mandelstam had been more on top of things he might have noticed the runs in Mama Celeste's stockings, how spotty her coat was. He would've discerned the wrinkles in her weathered face and memorized the macabre shape of her orthopedic shoes and the hem of her dress as it unraveled in an exodus of loose threads. He might have wondered what was in the shoebox. But no matter how savvy the cop might have been, he'd never have deduced, not in a thousand years, that she was a millionaire living in a tenement hotel. He queried her, "What's your name?"

"I'm Mama Celeste."

"Where do you live?"

Mama squeezed the shoebox to her bosom. "The Allen Hotel."

"And what are you doing here?"

"Getting me some coffee, maybe a jelly doughnut."

"You seen anything out of the ordinary around here? We had a robbery earlier this morning."

"I ain't seen nothing," Mama said stoutly.

There had been a time, like yesterday, when she hadn't been able to afford an aspirin for her sciatica. Money was like poor arithmetic. So many people had none. Others had too much. There was no balance in between. Now she had more money than city hall, more money than a rock star. Now she could afford a proper burial when the occasion arose.

Each step Mama Celeste executed might be her last one. When you were seventy-nine years old, you had to think like that. Forget the past. Forget the future. It was too confusing. It was better to stay focused on the present to make it last a smidgen longer.

Mortified that the shoebox was broadcasting the money in it, Mama ducked her head. The cook sensed her fear and moved back as Mandelstam raked him with tombstone eyes. The policeman's unblinking narcoleptic stare was hypnotic. He wasn't physically intimidating like other officers. He didn't swagger. He didn't bully. He just looked into you as if he knew everything that you were thinking.

Mandelstam guessed the old lady was lying, but as quickly as he felt the hunch, it vanished and he couldn't summon it again. The cook, watching him closely, relaxed and went back to his chores. He turned over the French fries on the stove and hurled a batch of hamburgers in the sink to thaw.

Maybe it was the music, that Tony Bennett, but Mandelstam was unable to focus. He was too damn tired. Rubbing his eyes, he had a flashback about a party he went to as a kid. He'd been dressed up in his best clothes, a pearl-buttoned cowboy outfit with rhinestones. After getting him to join a ring of other children underneath a papier mâché piñata in the living room, his father sauntered off to flirt with the host's wife. She was in the kitchen mixing up martinis for the adults.

The piñata was a crudely fashioned donkey that had been painted green. It was attached to a fixture on the ceiling by a garden rope. The birthday girl, a tow-headed rug rat in a pink dress, announced to everyone that they were going to play a game in her honor. The girl's daddy handed out plastic baseball bats to the kids assembled under the donkey. The object of the contest was to break the piñata and get at the toys inside it.

Armed with a bat, Mandelstam bashed the piñata into smithereens. A plethora of individually wrapped toys plummeted to the floor. He set his eyes on a black plastic gun and beat everyone to it. The gun was a replica of a Russian AK-47 assault rifle, just what he'd wanted.

This pissed off the birthday girl to no end. She freaked out and hollered that the plastic rifle was hers. She stamped her foot and chanted, give me the gun, give me the gun. The rest of the kids joined the chorus. Give her the gun. Give her the gun. The hue and cry grew louder. Mandelstam's semidrunken father and the girl's mother intervened; the toy was torn from his grubby mitts.

His father was in an Eddie Bauer chamois hunting shirt unbuttoned to his navel, and he upbraided Mandelstam in front of the other children. "What the fuck is wrong with you, boy? Don't you know how to share?"

Sequestered by his beery-smelling old man and the lady of the house, Mandelstam was escorted out of the living room and marched downstairs into a half-finished basement. The woman opened the door to a vacant laundry room. A little tipsy, she had lipstick all over her teeth. A barrette in her hair was about to drop off. She said, "In here, shrimp."

Mandelstam blubbered in his own defense. "But I didn't do nothing to no one."

Without further ado, he was deposited in the laundry room. His pops said, "I hope you'll learn something from this, kiddo." The door was shut with a resounding click of the lock. When the party was over, Mandelstam was released from confinement and his father drove him home.

A Neil Diamond tune came on the coffee shop's sound system; the opening bars of "Solitary Man" jarred the cop from his stupor. Mandelstam loved the song and remembered it well but had heard it too many times and didn't want to hear it again. He stiffened, nodded at Mama Celeste, turned around, and booked out the door and into the streets.

The cook waited until they were alone before saying to Mama, "I thought that whitey-ass old chump would never leave."

Mama took a deep breath. "The man was pesky, all right."

"He was looking at your shoebox. What you got in it?"

"Money."

It was the funniest thing the cook had heard all week. "Girl, you strictly from hunger," he said. "You ain't even got a penny." Laughing as if he was in on the joke, he shucked, "And what you doing with that money?"

"Whatever God tells me to do with it."

It was ten o'clock. Four hours had passed since the Brinks robbery. The rain had moved north over the Golden Gate Bridge into the coastal hills of Marin County. The soup kitchens in the Tenderloin were in full swing. Market Street's sidewalks were thick with burglars, dope fiends, prostitutes, and panhandlers. Mama Celeste had to get going.

FOUR

A DOVE SAT ON A TELEPHONE POLE at the corner of Van Ness and Market. It heard a mighty flapping of wings, looked to see what kind of bird was making the noise, and was attacked by a red-tailed hawk. The predator sank its talons in the dove's neck and yanked it from the pole. Flying off with the stunned creature, the hawk zoomed over the New College law school campus on Fell Street.

Richard Rood looked up at the red-tailed hawk and then at his fake Rolex watch. It was ten-thirty. On a scale of one to twenty, his day was starting out at zero. He had no food in his belly. No real money in his pockets. No weed to smoke. Leaning against a chain-link fence, he collected his thoughts. Stiv Wilkins had failed to come up with the money he owed. The white boy was a poltroon.

On the upside of things, Stiv was going to have to pay a harsh penalty for his transgression. Sadistic by nature, Richard looked forward to the thrill of punishing him. Maybe he'd beat Stiv into a pulp. Or put out a lit cigarette in his face. Cutting off the punk's ears with a knife sounded divine.

If it hadn't been for the black-and-white police cruiser that pulled up beside him, Richard Rood would've stood there all day thinking on how to torture Stiv Wilkins. The car announced itself by backfiring, emitting a report identical to the discharge of a large caliber hand-gun. Officer Mandelstam turned off the engine and decamped from the vehicle in slow motion, as if he were losing a battle with gravity.

A stainless steel Ruger Security Six revolver in a lightweight canvas mesh holster was glued to his hip. A four-foot-long plastic nightstick with a whiplash handle was in his gloved fist.

Richard Rood assessed the cop and was mellow. He wasn't sweating it. He had no warrants out on him. No outstanding tickets to pay. No probation violations hanging over his head. He wasn't going to get busted, not for no penny-ante shit. He wasn't holding any drugs. No dime bags of indica. No bags of crank. No stolen credit cards. No guns or knives. He was clean, pure as driven snow. Which was wise because his rap sheet was sizable—a grand total of thirty-seven arrests that had resulted in two felony convictions and ten years of court-appointed probation. But staying clean also meant he wasn't doing any trade. Which meant Richard had no cash.

"All right," Mandelstam burped, "what are you doing?"

Richard folded his arms, haughtily stuck his nose in the air, and said, "Not a damn thing. I'm out here being all copacetic, enjoying the weather."

"That'll be the day. Bring yourself and that fucking red suit you got on over here to the car."

The black dealer felt his temper go up a notch. "What for?"

"Because you and I are going to have a tête-à-tête." The policeman palmed the nightstick. "Empty out your pockets, shit for brains. Then put your hands on the hood where I can see them."

There was a time for resisting arrest and there was a time to submit to a frisk. There was a time for getting thrashed with a nightstick. There was a time for going to jail. And there was a time for calling your bondsman to raise bail. There was a time for everything under the sun. It occurred to Richard Rood this wasn't a time to fuck around with Mandelstam. He removed his alligator-skin billfold from his pants, threw it on the ground, and deployed his hands on the black-and-white's hood.

"Spread your legs," Mandelstam said. "I want to see daylight."

Rifling the dealer's jacket pockets, the cop found a pencil, a pack of chewing gum, a ring of keys, an address book with nobody's name in it, and the measly five dollars that Richard had to his name. With a cheerful grin—now he had cigarette money for the day—Mandelstam tucked the bill in his belt and commented, "Nice suit you got on. You look like a fucking ghetto Santa Claus in it."

Richard pivoted, looked over his shoulder at Mandelstam. "Say who?"

Mandelstam continued the pat down, running his fingers over Richard's pants. He came up with a deck of pornographic playing cards, two half-smoked cigarette butts, a nail clipper, and a book of matches. He searched Richard's legs, pulling down his socks, and copped a bottle of Vicodin. The policeman had a horselaugh at his discovery. He read the label and said, "Fucking opiates. I love them. This stuff gets you so blitzed and constipated, I took it for my legs once and I didn't have a bowel movement for six days. I didn't know if I was in heaven or hell."

The carrot-faced cop was convinced the black man was a junkie. The evidence was the red suit. Richard Rood had to be an addict with that kind of taste in clothes. The only people who wore loud colors in the Tenderloin were dope fiends and whores. "What you taking the Vicodin for?" he asked.

"Doctor's orders."

"Yeah, right. And the Pope smokes dope. Let's see your arms."

Richard rolled back the sleeves of his jacket with dignity. The cop studied his shiny black skin with the zealotry of a rocket scientist and was visibly angered when he didn't find any telltale tracks. For Richard the worst part of the ordeal wasn't having his money taken. It wasn't having his nuts fondled by Mandelstam. It wasn't having his Vicodin stolen. And it wasn't having his suit ridiculed. It was the cloying scent of Mandelstam's deodorant. The smell had managed to get in his jheri curls. He was standing so close to the white dude, he could see every pore on his cauliflower nose, even the blackheads that ringed his nostrils.

"You're on drugs." Mandelstam held the Vicodin bottle up to the sun to prove his thesis. "What do you know about the Brinks money?"

Richard deflected the interrogative. He didn't know what the cop was talking about. "What money?"

Mandelstam's riot helmet refracted the sun's etiolated rays. "Don't give me that crap, you asshole," he said. "You're out here all day long. You know what I'm talking about."

An asshole was uncool. An asshole was dishonest. An asshole was a perjurer and a back-stabber. An asshole hedged his bets. It was the cruelest of insults. Gnashing his teeth, Richard Rood resisted the urge to sass the policeman. Much as he wanted to start a fight, he saw the wisdom in keeping his trap shut. There was no sense in causing aggravation or a fracas. He didn't want to get on the receiving end of the nightstick. He didn't want to go to the hoosegow. He didn't want to sit in a felony tank cell with nothing to do, and so he was deliberate with his answer. "I don't know a thing about no goddamn money."

Richard was telling the truth. He didn't know squat about the Brinks paper. But it was plain to see by the scornful look on Mandelstam's mug that honesty would get him nowhere. The realization was bitter and deepened his belief that lying was the only way to get through life.

Mandelstam trained the nightstick on him. "My ass, you don't. You're probably the dick who ran off with it. Where else would you get the cash to buy that shitty vinyl suit you got on?"

Rood was taken aback. Bile rose in his throat. Pink lights danced behind his eyes. The punk was saying his suit was made from plastic? He would allow no man or beast to disrespect his vines. He'd paid four hundred dollars for them at Kaplan's army-navy surplus store. The cop had crossed his Rubicon—he just didn't know it yet. Richard cursed him softly, "Fuck you, man. If I had that Brinks money, you think I'd be out here dealing with your shit? Hell, no. I'd be in a penthouse, kicking back in style."

His opinion hung uncomfortably in the air. It hadn't been a smart thing to say. The sentiment guaranteed him a trip into a wilderness of misery. The words had barely escaped from his mouth when he had to deal with the cop's response.

Each policeman utilizes a nightstick differently. Some use an overhead approach. Others swing it like a bat. Still more policemen wield their billy clubs as if it was a pike. Mandelstam had been schooled in the traditional thrust and jab technique. Quick as a snake, he peppered Richard Rood's ribcage with the tip of the stick.

It was curtains for Richard. His legs gave out, and he couldn't swallow. He turned blue in the face and his eyes did a circuit in their sockets. Then he collapsed to the pavement, and had a flash through the pain about the first man he'd ever kissed.

Armed with a forged identification card, he'd been hanging out in a Fillmore district bar. The neighborhood was a historic black community that had been ninety square blocks before gentrification whittled it down to nil. An older hustler in a dapper silk suit motioned for Richard to join him. They smoked a medium-sized joint in the back by the pool tables and talked about the people they knew in common. It so happened the dude knew Richard's mother. After a while they ran out of things to say. The hustler put his hand on Richard's shoulder, turned his head so that his face was shining white from a lamp. He hooked his other hand behind Richard's neck and drew him close. He gently kissed the younger man's lower lip, saying, "That's nice, ain't it?"

Richard's face rushed to meet the ground. His last meal, clam chowder and a Greek salad with an espresso from the deli on Ellis Street, gushed out of his mouth and splashed down his suit. He went out like a light.

Rood roused himself five minutes later. His head was on the sidewalk and his legs were in the gutter. Pedestrians were walking around him, making as if he wasn't there. He jackknifed to his feet, got his billfold and slipped it back in his jacket. Getting harassed by the police was no big deal. But it killed his spirit every time. Like he was a square of toilet paper they could wipe themselves on. That cop was going to suffer for messing with him. Richard brushed off his pants and jacket and made a decision. He was done waiting for his money. It was time to proceed to phase two of his plan. He had reached a verdict: track down Stiv Wilkins and regain what he was owed.

The problem was, the task wouldn't be simple. It required a strategy, an umbrella of ideas that fit together. Richard had his limits. He had his phobias. The nitty-gritty was he didn't want to leave his patch. The strip of Market Street between Van Ness Avenue and Octavia Street was all he had.

Whenever he left the four blocks that constituted his universe, Richard felt as if he was heading off-planet. Traveling to a foreign solar system. What with all the trouble going down, the cops acting loco about the Brinks money, things were just too hot. So he had a decision to make. Was the four hundred dollars worth the effort?

The clock tower above the Goodwill store on Mission Street said it was a few minutes after eleven. Richard peered up the road at the Allen Hotel. That's where Stiv lived in a room no bigger than a refrigerator. The walk to the Allen was lengthy, maybe three blocks. A journey that was too long for a man of Richard's importance.

He couldn't be seen walking around like some low-rent dunce—his credibility was at stake. His stature would be diminished if anyone saw him taking a stroll to the Allen. Only suckers and folks with no class tooled up Market Street on foot. Beggars, panhandlers, winos, and junkies walked. The better classes drove cars. But the debt had to be collected.

Richard recalled something he'd heard about Stiv, some gossip. Hearsay about a woman the punk was involved with, the wife of a dope dealer. That made him even angrier. He had no use for women, including any that were connected to Stiv Wilkins.

Fighting the wind, he began his march to the Allen Hotel.

Mama Celeste flailed past him going the opposite way on Market Street. Her left shoe was untied. The baseball hat was cocked at a jaunty angle. A stream of dreadlocks plunged down her shoulders. The army jungle coat rustled in the breeze as she walked. Talking out loud to herself, she didn't see the frowning black man in the red patent leather suit.

Richard Rood recoiled, narrowly avoiding a collision with her. His nose was running. He had goose bumps up and down his back from the flu. His mouth tasted of vomit. A cop had taken his money and his Vicodin. An old biddy with a beat-up Reebok shoebox was the last thing he needed to lay eyes on.

"Damn crone," he lamented. "Ought to be in a rest home and shit."

FIVE

WHILE SHARONA SUNBATHED on the hotel roof with the baby, Stiv sat on the bed in their room and dry-shaved himself with a disposable razor. Having no mirror or shaving cream, he did it by feel, gliding the blade across his chin. Sweat glittered on his forearms. His big boned feet were pronated, the toe nails yellow and uncut. His eyes were glacier-blue and heated. He finished the task with a couple of bloody swipes at his neck.

He put his toiletries in the sink, got down on his hands and knees, and ferreted a tartan-red suitcase out from under the bed frame. He unzipped the case and removed two handguns. The first gat was a generic Saturday night special. The other weapon was a Colt revolver. He dusted off both guns with a handkerchief and put them on the window's sill. His intention was to sell the Saturday night special.

Needing to pee, he lumbered out of the room and trod barefoot through the gloomy hall to use the communal toilet. The overhead water pipes were clanging. The walls swayed from the traffic on Market Street. The carpet was treacherous and he managed to avoid stepping on a gargantuan cockroach. Stiv went up a flight of wobbly stairs and almost collided with Jeeter Roche's wife.

Gussied up in a floral-patterned muumuu dress and eight-inch white leatherette platform shoes, Chiclet Dupont had her business face on, replete with a titanic embellishment of mascara and rouge. She carried a notepad in one hand. A pen was tucked behind her ear.

A clove cigarette was sticking out of her mouth. A Dell laptop in a Barnes and Noble book bag was slung over her shoulder. She was in the process of collecting rent from the tenants.

"Good morning, doll," he said. "What's up with you?"

The platforms gave Chiclet a ten-inch advantage in height over Stiv. She was courteous, but reserved: he wasn't the only person having doubts about their relationship. She said, "The same as usual. I'm getting the rent money from everyone. You got yours for me?"

He was vague. "Uh, not yet."

"You aren't going to be late with it, are you?"

"No, of course not," he said hastily. "I'm good for it."

"I hope so. Jeeter gets weird otherwise and then he takes it out on me."

Stiv played it smart and didn't say anything about his money problems. Chiclet wouldn't want to hear it. The mere mention of it would turn her against him. She didn't like her men weak. But Stiv had a plan and he needed to meet with Jeeter. Was this an appropriate time to bring it up? He wasn't sure—the dank passageway was so impersonal. But he forced himself to do it. "Tell me," he inveigled, "you doing anything?"

"Why?"

"You got any weed?"

Chiclet looked down her nose at Stiv. "What for?"

"I want to get smoked out. I'm stressing something ugly."

Getting high wasn't a bad idea. But business took priority. Chiclet held up the notepad, letting frustration colorize her voice. "I can't smoke no dope now. I'm getting revenue for Jeeter. It's rent day, damn it. You know how he is. He watches every penny. And you better have your check for me soon."

Stiv hated being hounded for the rent—he was no better off than a hamster on a treadmill. "Yeah, sure, later," he said. "Give me a couple of hours." He lifted his arms. As the elastic in his lime-green boxer shorts was stretched out, the motion caused the underwear to slide off his bony hips and drop to the floor. His pimpled buttocks were luminous in the hallway's murk. He put a hand on Chiclet's arm and said, "Listen."

Literal-minded Chiclet didn't hear anything. The hall was as silent as a cemetery. She said, "Listen to what?"

"No, no, listen to me. I want to see Jeeter."

"What for?"

"I've got a deal for him."

Chiclet wasn't enthused. "We don't need any more drugs, Stiv. We have everything under the goddamn sun."

"It ain't drugs that I'm talking about."

"Yeah? What is it then?"

"I have something extra special."

She was wary. "Oh?"

"Yeah. A piece."

"A gun?"

"Yup. Cheap, too."

Chiclet was solemn. She thought about Stiv's proposal for a moment, running it through the corners of her mind. She saw nothing wrong with it, saying, "You're in luck. Jeeter's been looking for one lately. I'll tell him you have something for him. Come on over in an hour. Can you do that?"

"Sure can."

"You know where we're living these days?"

"Near the Otis Street welfare office, right?"

"Right."

Chiclet bussed Stiv on the cheek and said good-bye. She proceeded downstairs to deliver an eviction notice to a tenant on the fourth floor. Stiv watched her descend the staircase and touched the spot on his skin where her lips had been. Then he pulled up his boxer shorts and went back to his room.

Getting dressed was easy. Stiv leaped into a pair of silver-buckled engineer boots, his favorite T-shirt, and the motorcycle jacket, and then stuffed the Saturday night special in his waistband. Leaving the room was harder. He opened the door, slithered into the hall, shut the door, and bolted the lock. He checked it, did it again, and two more times after that. He took a couple of steps toward the exit and went back to check the doorknob a fifth time. His agoraphobia was getting out of hand.

Tearing himself away, Stiv bounded down the rear stairs to the ground floor and burst out of the emergency exit onto the sidewalk. Walking in the tepid sunshine to the Muni bus stop at Franklin Street, he finished a joint, the last pinch of what he'd taken off Richard Rood.

A turn-of-the-century F-line car from the Castro pulled up to the stop. Jumping aboard, Stiv looked around the overcrowded carriage. The only vacant seat was in a compartment by a quartet of armed transit cops with two German shepherd guard dogs, and he decided not to sit down. The train conductor's disembodied voice wafted over the car's loudspeaker: "Next stop . . . Civic Center."

Rattling toward the Civic Center, the trolley pitched from side to side. One of the cops attempted to make eye contact with Stiv. He looked the other way and paid close attention to the street as it whizzed by the train. A Public Health Service ambulance was at the corner of Larkin and Market; medics were loading a homeless man onto a stretcher.

Getting Sharona pregnant had been a colossal accident. The stupid things you did when you were lonely were amazing. You'd sleep with anyone without a rubber on, so long as they were warm and breathing. And having a kid had become an error of monumental proportions. That became evident on the night the baby was born. Straight out of jail, Stiv visited Sharona and the brat in the welfare maternity ward at General Hospital.

Holding the pointy-headed creature that was supposed to be their son in the crook of her elbow, Sharona said to Stiv, honeyed and dulcet-toned, "I need to tell you something."

The triumph in her voice made Stiv paranoid. "What is it?"

"You have to become a responsible parental figure."

She might as well have been speaking in Hebrew. He said, "What in the hell are you barking at?"

"It's like this," Sharona lectured. "Are you going to be a daddy or a father?"

It was mumbo-jumbo in his ears. "Huh?"

"A daddy just hangs around. A father goes out and gets a job and takes care of his family."

Sharona's edict had been a major bring-down. Stiv had never met his own father, didn't even know the man's name, so what the fuck was she saying? He didn't have a clue. Here he was, twenty-five years old, fathering a child way too soon. Now he had to step up to the plate for Sharona and the kid and deliver the things he'd never known.

The trolley shuddered to a halt at the Civic Center station and the coach doors opened. Stiv disembarked and muscled a path through knots of school kids, junkies, suited office workers, and Nicaraguan women selling food. The line of passengers struggling to get out of the station was lengthy. A surveillance camera embedded in a wall gazed unblinkingly at the crowd. Keeping an eye on two overweight Muni cops guarding the entrance, Stiv cut to the front, bestraddled a turnstile, and hopped over it.

A ticket agent shouted at him, "Hey! You didn't pay!"

Stiv jogged across Market Street. Resurgent wisps of fog wreathed the eucalyptus trees and the hillside condominiums on Diamond Heights. A red, white, and blue zeppelin bobbled over the office buildings in the Tenderloin. The weekly farmer's market was in progress at the Civic Center. Azure blue and orangeade yellow clouds hovered over the gray government buildings in the plaza.

The neighborhood where Jeeter Roche dwelled, the South of Market, was populated with live-work lofts, high-rise retirement complexes, shopping centers, factories, and warehouses. The writer Jack London had been born at Third and Brannan. The last comprehensive general strike in San Francisco had been organized here by the ILWU in 1934. The district had been a hub for book printing on the West Coast, but skyrocketing production costs had driven the industry overseas to Korea and Singapore.

The South of Market was also a haven for the city's leather queens. Bars like the Brig and the Anvil on Folsom Street attracted large mobs on the weekends. Stiv had frequented the Brig; his streetwise scruffiness was irresistible to the leather daddies. One of them, a queen by the name of Robert Opel, developed a crush on him. Usually done up in a black leather vest and chaps and pale-faced with a bushy mustache that masked his sardonic mouth, Robert promoted an ego that took up a lot of room. He'd streaked the Oscar Awards on national television and had become a celebrity. He had a flair for making the people around him seem smaller than they were. The attribute left more than one person wanting to murder him.

History doesn't repeat itself; it merely predicts what's been done before. Robert Opel got involved with the wrong people and was shot and killed in a PCP deal that went south. A pimply-faced queen was busted for the deed. One day while going to a preliminary hearing at the Hall of Justice, the shooter escaped from the holding cell next to the courtroom. Dressed in a pair of orange county-jail overalls, he evaded the cops and vamoosed all the way to Florida before he was captured again. Stiv stayed away from the Brig after that.

Walking by the warehouses on Howard Street, he was aware that the residual effects of the Haldol had worn off. His head was clearer than it had been all morning. His hearing was more acute. His sight was stronger. His ability to smell was enhanced. It wouldn't be long before he had another hallucination.

Hallucinations had a herd mentality. They ran in packs. You had one, others joined in to gangbang your nervous system. Stiv got a hint of things to come when he spotted the wraith of José Reyna on Tehama Street. The outlaw was gauzy, transparent in the sunlight. He was in the saddle of a white stallion. The horse, a muscular brute, reared up on its hind legs and neighed. José waved his sombrero. The poltergeist lasted for all two seconds, enough to worry Stiv.

SIX

JEETER ROCHE'S HOME was in a refurbished twelve-unit Victorian apartment house in Stevenson Alley. Recently painted a pastel blue, the building had a FOR SALE sign on the front door. Stiv rang the bell and was let in through the security gate. Going inside, he had a glimpse of his reflection in the lobby's mirror. His posture was that of a man who was ill at ease. Plastic frame sunglasses hid his eyes. His hips and legs were toothpicks, smaller than his chest and shoulders. His hair was slick and black. His complexion was gray from the Allen Hotel lifestyle. "You look like shit," Stiv said to the mirror.

He went upstairs to the fifth floor. A potted palm tree stood sentry in the hall next to a window. The door to Jeeter's apartment was ajar, and without knocking, Stiv slouched into the place. He tramped through a vestibule reeking with incense into an airy, spacious living room. Five dormer windows let in lukewarm light from the noisy alley.

The walls were packed with bookshelves; paperback novels spilled onto the floor. A Random House dictionary sat on the coffee table, along with a moth-eaten softback copy of Boris Pasternak's *Doctor Zhivago*. Beached on a brown lizard-skin sofa were Jeeter Roche and Chiclet Dupont. Jeeter's pupils were the size of silver dollars. Psychedelic mushrooms, Stiv guessed.

Jeeter savaged Stiv with a dismissive glance. Speaking in a queeny deadpan, the voice he used when relating to an inferior, he tapped

Chiclet on the knee with a nail-bitten finger and said, "What the fuck is going on? You didn't tell me Stiv Wilkins was coming over. What's up with that? You trying to get me all freaked out and shit? I am unprepared for this. I do not feel in control."

Chiclet fidgeted, a twitch that was exaggerated by the two five-milligram Valiums she'd just taken. She was in the zone where she was getting high, but not fast enough, and protested with vigor. "I did too tell you, Jeeter, damn it. You weren't fucking listening."

Stiv removed his motorcycle jacket and swung it over his shoulder. His steel-toed engineer boots scuffed the hardwood floor. He hooked his thumbs in his belt loops, rested his weight on one leg, and challenged Jeeter with a snarl, "You got a problem with me being here? I can leave if you want."

Jeeter's eyes were dark with the promise of conflict. His forehead was punctuated with a rill of tension. His overdeveloped arms strained against the sleeves of a hemp-fiber yoga shirt. His feet were bare and missing two toes. He dropped the book he'd been reading, Bernard Malamud's *The Natural,* and said, "No, man, it's cool. I'm not sweating you. Just checking out what comes in the door, you know what I'm saying?"

"I heard that."

"Damn right, dude. Have a seat."

Acknowledging Stiv with a wan smile, Chiclet was curled up in the sofa's pads. She was clad in a polyester imitation sarong and an orange suede halter-top, and her hair was dyed bright cadmium yellow. In the late morning light her unlined, pockmarked face was ashen from a lack of sleep. A tic was working overtime on her right cheek. She was busily picking at the scabs on her newly tattooed forearms.

The living room was equipped with a pair of overstuffed velveteen chairs, white woolen drapes, walnut bookshelves from IKEA, an ersatz Turkish carpet, and a solid glass side table. A boom box on the table burbled a report about the Brinks money case. The police were now saying that, pending further notice, information to the public would be limited.

Stiv brushed a book of Picasso prints from a chair, deposited himself in the cushions, and made polite talk. "Fine place you got here. Pretty swell."

Jeeter's face was puffy and pallid; his lips were scarlet red and glistened with saliva. He accepted the compliment with typical gracelessness. "I've been doing real well this year. Selling weed is booming." He confirmed this with Chiclet. "Ain't that right, honey?"

Chiclet uncrossed her legs and started to get up. "That's right, Jeeter." She adjusted her halter-top, giving both men a candid shot of her alabaster breasts. She said to Stiv, "You want something to drink? We've got filtered water, beer, and Pepsi. Or you want to smoke a joint?" Her flat eyes sparkled. "I'll roll a fatty with this here primo Canadian bud we've got."

Jeeter motioned for her to sit back down, holding his hand up, palm out. His muscle-bound body radiated excitement and disharmony. He said with a slur, "Later with the smoke. We're doing business, darling."

Chiclet flushed, the pocks on her cheeks lighting up with embarrassment. "Gosh, I'm sorry."

Ignoring his wife, Jeeter riveted Stiv with a paranoid stare, giving his guest a sample of his prison glare. It was a grimace that he'd acquired during a six-year stay in San Quentin. He didn't say a word, just looked bald and mean. Then he asked, "So you brought me a cheap piece? Something inexpensive?"

Stiv got cocky. "Yeah, I did. The cream of the crop."

Jeeter said, "I'm pleased to hear that, mighty pleased. Show me what you've got."

Parting his jacket, Stiv dragged out the Saturday night special from his belt. It was a chrome-plated .25 caliber eight-shot semiautomatic that could fit in a child's palm. The grips were mother-of-pearl. The finish around the pistol's muzzle was tarnished. The barrel had nicks all over it. The gun's appearance let you know that it would blow up in your eyes when you put your finger on the trigger. Not worth more than twenty bucks in the street, its only virtue was in being concealable, which made it an excellent tool for crime.

Stiv said with a straight face, "It's a beauty, ain't it? *La mera mata. The real deal.*"

Hearing the Spanish, Jeeter brightened. "You're bilingual, ain't you?"

"I'm not," Stiv said. "I'm from Oregon. From Portland."

Jeeter eyeballed the pistol. His doughy features were impossible to read. There was no color in his cheeks and no zest in his eyes. You would've never known he was alive if it hadn't been for his lips, which wouldn't stop moving. He said, "Please, let me see that thing."

Handing the weapon to him, Stiv said, "This is the finest you can get, guaranteed."

Jeeter scoffed. "Don't be ridiculous, Stiv. It looks old."

"It ain't."

Hefting the gat, Jeeter aimed it at the floor. He aimed it at the ceiling. He aimed it at Chiclet. He aimed it at Stiv. Pointing the gun at himself, he pressed the trigger five times in rapid succession. The firing pin sounded no more substantial than a paper clip and there weren't any bullets in the magazine. The bullets—slugs that were no bigger than a grown man's thumbnail—would cost Jeeter extra. They were a dollar apiece and were in Stiv's pocket.

Three vertical lines terraced Jeeter's brow. There was a question mark grooved in his tightened lips. You could see the dollar signs in his bookworm eyes, how he was already angling to drive the asking price downward. He stuck his tongue out and blew a raspberry. "It ain't hot, is it?" he asked. "I want a clean gun."

All guns are born with a blank slate. The Saturday night special had a legacy. It had been used by a junkie acquaintance of Stiv's to rob liquor stores in the Tenderloin, the last one being at Turk and Hyde. During the heist, the junkie, suffering from withdrawals, had panicked and fired several shots at the clerk. The bullets took out a Gallo wine display case. The robber's face and the gun were captured on video—the police were searching everywhere for him and the weapon. So he unloaded the pistol on Stiv for ten dollars.

Stiv was getting desperate and lied to Jeeter without remorse. The truth would get him zip. Nor would it earn him any money. "It's fresh from the manufacturers. Never been used for nothing. It's virgin."

"You sure? It doesn't look it." Jeeter toyed with the pistol, turning it over in his hand. He said to Chiclet, "What do you think, babe?"

An artificial smile flickered on his wife's mouth and died in her eyes. The rictus enslaved her face in a harlequin's grin. Chiclet didn't know anything about weapons, and she was getting too high to care. "Buy it if you want it, sugar. Just make sure it's a deal."

A scowl crossed Jeeter's irregular features. "It ain't right."

Stiv would've been retarded if he hadn't noticed Jeeter's hesitation. He said, "What ain't?"

Jeeter baited him. "The gun, damn it. It don't look new to me, man. I'll give you fifty bucks for it. That's a fair price."

"Fifty dollars?" Stiv snorted. "You're fucking unreal. Shit, it's worth at least a hundred."

"No way. You're fantasizing. I'll give you fifty. No more than that."

Stiv whinnied, "Unh uh, cowboy. You have to give me at least sixty-five bones."

"I can't do that," Jeeter complained. "I'm already being too generous. You have to lighten up on the price tag. You know me . . . I can get anything, anytime, anywhere. If you don't give me what I want, someone else will. Now you want to do this thing or not?"

"You're taking advantage of my largesse." Stiv got sulky. "I'm only asking for sixty-five shitty bucks. That's chicken feed to a player like you."

Jeeter rasped, "Fifty dollars. That's my final offer. Take it or leave it."

Stiv pleaded. "How about sixty-four?"

"Nope. You're way off."

"Sixty-three?"

"Not in this lifetime."

"Sixty-two?"

Jeeter smiled. "You're out of my league."

"Sixty-one."

"You're getting closer."

"Sixty?"

"Keep coming down."

"Fifty-nine?"

Jeeter hunched his shoulders and said earnestly, "Can't do it."

"Fifty-eight?"

"No."

"Fifty-seven?"

"No."

"Jesus Christ, you're killing me. Fifty-six?"

"Nope."

Chiclet begged Stiv's case with Jeeter. The Valium was finally hitting, charging her with a blast of unfocused energy. She bent forward on the couch, elbows on her knees, hair in her eyes. "Sweetie, let's give him five extra dollars. I have it in my purse. Stiv's got a baby and shit to deal with. He needs whatever he can get his hands on."

Jeeter didn't tolerate kibitzing from the sidelines. Buying guns wasn't a spectator sport. It was for seasoned men only. He whirled on Chiclet; his cheeks were eggplant purple from hypertension. "You hush up, chick. This is commerce. It ain't welfare."

"Fifty-five bucks, Jeeter, c'mon," Stiv cajoled.

"No, fifty."

Stiv was galled. He was doubtful and said, "I don't know about this."

Jeeter pointed the Saturday night special at Stiv. He put his other arm around Chiclet's shoulders and snuggled her to his chest. He quipped, "What's there not to know? Think of it this way. You have something and I want it. It's a war of wills. Now what's it going be. Fifty dollars or nothing?"

Smelling Jeeter's feet from where he sat, Stiv said, "Fifty bucks?"

"You heard me right, bucko. Take it or leave it."

Stiv was disappointed. His whole life it had been like this, big fish eating the little fish. There were only two kinds of people in the world, winners and losers. He had the dreadful feeling he was in the second category. "I'll take it."

Payment was five shabby ten-dollar bills—even Jeeter's money was insulting. Stiv had half a mind to ask him if the cash had been dug up from a grave. The bills stank of death and decay. But he kept his opinion to himself. There was no point in egging on the bastard. You were only asking for more damage. He waltzed to his feet, smiled icily at his hosts, and said, "Nice doing business with you. I'll let myself out."

Heading home to the Allen Hotel, Stiv swung over to Market Street. He sauntered by the fashionable Zuni Café. Smart little tables with crisp white tablecloths had been set up on the sidewalk to take advantage of the Indian summer weather. Patrons resplendent in chic black business suits were eating and drinking while waiters bustled to and from the bar.

A hundred yards away from the café was a homeless encampment. In the center of the camp a man was asleep. Surrounded by cardboard and goose down sleeping bags, he was enjoying the sunshine. His young-old face was serene. His pencil-thin legs were crossed, and his feet were emblazoned with bloodstains. His wrists bore the marks of recent contusions. A circus of green flies whirled around his head. Buried in rags, he was no more substantial than a pile of leaves fallen from a tree. A tiny sparrow with brown wings and a fluted beak pecked at the blood on his feet.

The civil defense siren went off, as it did every Tuesday at noon.

The Brinks money had been gone for six hours.

SEVEN

RICHARD ROOD GAVE the farmer's market in the Civic Center a hard look. The brick-paved plaza was swamped with sea gulls. Winos were sitting by the fountain. Senior citizens from Chinatown swarmed around merchants selling Fuji apples from Sonoma, mushrooms from Mendocino, fish from the bay, and almonds harvested near Firebaugh.

The place gave Richard the creeps. It reminded him of his days as a drag queen. Back when he was a man-child in an ash blonde wig, a satin gown, and a cashmere stole, hustling businessmen from suburban Marin in the bars on Geary Street.

He was in a dive one night in 1979, a balmy May evening with no fog or wind. Spring was only a week long in the city and Richard had been enjoying the rare warm weather. A guy came in, ordered a whiskey with water, and said the faggots were rioting on Market Street because of Dan White.

A former policeman turned politician, Dan White was from a working-class neighborhood known as Visitacion Valley. He had shot and killed the mayor and a gay public official at city hall the previous November. He had been put on trial for two counts of first-degree murder, but the jury had let him off easy, and he was sentenced to eight years in prison.

Hearing the news, Richard ran down the hill from Geary in his stocking feet, holding his high heels in one hand. At the corner of Turk, drag queens were trashing a liquor store. The ground floor windows of the State Building on McAllister had been wrecked. Eleven police cars in a row were burning in the Civic Center. Sirens were going off. Windshields were exploding. Richard skipped over to the first cop car in the line, broiling inside a casket of flames. He tore the wig from his scalp and threw it in the fire.

That had been a long time ago. He was different now. Wasn't a womanish boy, didn't get up in drag. Didn't waste his time stealing from drunken old white men in bars. The town had changed along with him. You just can't kill the mayor without a backlash. There was less housing, no jobs, and a permanent army of homeless.

Wending past a fruit stall laden with twenty-pound bags of oranges, Rood drifted through the Civic Center to Market Street. An assortment of police vehicles, several battered vans, three bullet-pocked Humvees, and a dozen patrol cars, barricaded the boulevard's four lanes. A repairman in an asbestos jumpsuit was climbing a ladder to rewire the telephone lines that had fallen down during the Brinks crashing. A platoon of cops in powder blue combat overalls and white riot helmets were stationed behind a sandbagged control point at a Muni bus stop.

Standing at the curb, Richard was infuriated. The scar on his forehead was tender. His radar was up. There were just too many police in the street. Made him feel like a rat in a cage. He thumped his chest with a fist. No way in hell was he going to let them get him. He hoofed it down the block toward Sixth Street. An aged wino in a mackinaw called out to him from a porno shop doorway, singing, "Young blood, you got any spare change for a brother?"

Richard wagged his grizzled head at the wino. "I ain't got shit, homes. The cops done took my last cent."

The sidewalks were lathered with tourists, guys in wheelchairs selling candles, homeless kids and their dogs, businesspeople going to lunch in the smorgasbords on Kearney Street. Richard pondered the money that Stiv Wilkins owed him. The punk was making it hard to get.

Vigilance had kept the cops and his enemies off Richard's back. But vigilance was a loan shark that demanded too much of his spirit. Made him so persnickety, he wanted to scream in terror. And terror had caused him to kill three men. One fellow he'd snuffed with a handgun, dusting him from a distance, maybe ten yards, with a Charter Arms .44 six-shooter. The guy had been talking in a phone booth, calling the police. Richard hadn't felt a thing when the bullet lopped off the stool pigeon's head and left his brains on the ground.

Killing a man with your bare hands—now that was slow-dancing with the lights turned low. Richard and another dope dealer had been in the restroom of the Stud on Ninth and Harrison. It was disco night. The disc jockey was playing vintage Thelma Houston. The floor had been crowded with dancers. The music drummed through the walls; the bass line had been wicked enough to loosen the fillings in Richard's teeth.

He'd sold the dealer a bag of fine-quality Colombian weed, a quarter ounce for a hundred dollars; the guy turned around to walk off without paying. Richard said, "What the fuck are you doing?" and the thief produced a stiletto. He menaced Richard, waving the knife as though it were a magic wand. Richard knocked the cutter from the man's hand and pushed him through a pair of toilet stall doors. He forced him onto his knees, rammed his face into a toilet bowl, and drowned him in two inches of water. His victim's final breath had been tart, like an unhappy lover's.

Richard glanced at his watch and winced. It was now one o'clock. Leaves jitterbugged on the ground. A chain-link fence rattled mournfully in the wind. A foghorn tooted in the bay. The hour promised two things: fog from the ocean, and more cops. The flu complicated matters. He'd never been so wasted in his life. Maybe he should get himself tested to see if he had a bug. Go down to the Public Health Service center on Lech Walesa Street and have a blood test.

He meandered into the crosswalk by the Warfield Theater and looked to his left. A cop car muddied from the rain was coming straight at him. He froze, not knowing which way to go. He looked east on Market Street and saw the police had blocked off traffic.

Some people when they see a policeman, they turn to stone. Others remember their lawyer's telephone number. Richard Rood high-jumped the mural-painted fence where the Embassy Theater used to be and dove head first into a vacant lot. Landing in a cesspool of rainwater, truck tires, and plastic garbage bags, he struggled to his feet and legged it through the lot into the mouth of Stevenson Alley.

The black-and-white turned the corner onto Seventh Street and was a hundred yards behind him. The cop car swerved into an over-turned trashcan and lost a hubcap. The driver floored the brakes to avoid a pothole, put the gears in reverse, then shifted into drive and gunned the gas pedal. The cruiser's oil pan scraped the roadbed; the trunk sprang open as the car bellied forward and raced through the alley at sixty miles per hour.

A garbage truck backed out of a warehouse loading dock, and the black-and-white cooked a brodie in the road, leaving a set of skid marks a hundred feet long, stopping inches short of a collision with the truck. A cloud of radiator steam rose from under the police car's blistered hood. Officer Mandelstam flung open the driver's door, unstrapped his riot helmet, and threw it on the gravel. He stared at Richard Rood as the black dealer skedaddled toward the alley's end.

Climbing a wooden fence, Richard pulled himself over the top and leapfrogged into an abandoned parking lot. Going full speed, he ran through a rent in the lot's fence onto Mission Street and then scrammed over to the Highway 101 overpass. Midway up the adjacent block, in between the Schwarz Sausage Co. factory and the Chevron gas station on Fourteenth Street, he found a man spread-eagled on the ground.

The dude was a middle-aged Mexican male in a Carhartt work vest. His pants were bunched around his hips. A pooling of blood had colored his crotch rust-red. He was shirtless; a row of deep knife cuts scored his skin. His stomach was lacerated and glistened with pinkish gore. Both of his shoes were missing, showing two bloody feet, one without socks. His biggest problem was the bullet hole in the side of his skull.

His head was turned to one side and his unseeing eyes gazed at the street with a look of hope and uncertainty. Newspapers surrounded the deceased, bullied by the wind. A sea gull winged away, squalling at what it had witnessed.

The sight of the dead man sent an electrical charge through Richard Rood. He recognized the sensation for what it was. Death was a summons. No more complex than getting a traffic ticket with a date to appear in court. Some people showed up when they were supposed to. Others didn't. If you were late, a warrant was issued for your arrest. Then you went to the underworld.

The doors of a motorcycle shop were open on the corner of Fourteenth Street. The blues song "You've Got to Love Her with a Feeling" by Freddie King swam onto the sidewalk. A car alarm sounded, followed by three more, melding into a choir. A heavyset crow in the street cawed at Richard. He craned his head and looked at the crow. The black bird was a scary sign: the day was going to get tougher before it got better.

EIGHT

SASHAYING UP MARKET STREET, Mama Celeste navigated the side-walk. The summer chill had settled in her feet no different than a winter in Siberia. The wind had reddened her cheeks. She looked at her face in the window of a parked car: her eyes were two balls filled with merciless self-consciousness. Her mouth was the entry wound on a murder victim. Her nose belonged to a survivor of self-hatred. It was the face of a stranger who knew everything about her. Mama couldn't bear to look any longer—enough was enough.

Mama wasn't sure how to distribute the money. Shading her eyes, she approached the intersection of Market and Valencia and recon-noitered it. A Department of Social Services parking lot was to one side. Up the street were the Baha'i Faith Center, the Zeitgeist bar, a liquor store, and a transmission repair shop.

Two homeless men were playing cards on a tarpaulin. The taller man had long black hair under a St. Louis Cardinals baseball hat. He was outfitted in a hippie-era fringed leather jacket and his legs were encased in a pair of filthy Calvin Klein stone-washed jeans. One leg was stretched out on the tarp; the other leg was a stump neatly pinned up at the thigh with a brooch. A pair of crutches lay across his lap. His buddy had a bandanna fashioned from a brown and red silk scarf. A green leather trench coat muffled his bony shoulders. He was cross-legged, intent on the cards.

A pit bull puppy tethered to a nearby shopping cart heard Mama and growled. The dude in the St. Louis baseball hat swiveled his head to see who it was. His gaunt oatmeal-white face went smooth when he saw the seal-brown woman. He opened his toothless mouth and gummed the words, "You looking for somebody, *chica*?"

The man in the bandanna looked up with milky blue eyes centered in a jet-black face and reached in his trench coat. He pulled out an unfiltered cigarette and a kitchen knife. He put the cigarette in his mouth and the knife on the tarp next to an army surplus sleeping bag. Turning to his friend, he pantomimed with his weather-beaten hands.

The fellow with one leg said to Mama Celeste, "My homeboy here is mute and he's saying you're making him nervous. What do you want from us?"

Mama made her move. Reaching in the shoebox, she plucked out a roll of hundreds. Hefting the cash in her palm, she said, "You all see this?"

The mute made the sign of the cross over himself and then put his hands over his ears and rocked back and forth. His partner, being inquisitive, tossed the cards on the tarp, adjusted the bill on his hat, and said to Mama, "Yeah, so? What's it got to do with me?"

Mama Celeste was holding twenty thousand dollars in legal tender. It was funny how the cash made everything prettier. The sunlight was brighter. The wind had an extra zing. Cars looked newer. The sky was a deeper shade of blue. Birds sang with greater zeal. The pavement was cleaner. Monarch butterflies zigzagged in and out of the palm trees. Even the garbage on the ground was nicer.

The stud in the baseball hat focused on the money and then on Mama Celeste. It took him a minute, but he figured it out. The lady with the dreadlocks was from the police. She was plainclothes, an undercover cop on a sting. Trying to lure him into a trap with the cash. Flapping a hand, he said to the mute, "Put the dog and the shit in the shopping cart and let's get the hell out of here."

Mama Celeste watched the two homeless men totter down Valencia Street. She replaced the money in the shoebox and moved off in the opposite direction. Fifty feet away from the crosswalk at McCoppin and Market she encountered a large sassy tomcat, a tangerine-colored tabby, sprawled out on a curbstone. The feline's whiskers were mangled. One of its ears was gone. Its eyes were green and sharp and took in Mama.

Only yesterday Mama had been a young woman. Married with a husband. Working for some friendly white folks in a rest home on Sutter Street. Went out dancing at the jazz clubs in the Fillmore on the weekend. Was saving a nest egg to buy a house in the suburbs out near Pinole in the East Bay. Everything in life had been ahead of her. Now all that was behind her.

On their honeymoon her husband had rented a car and driven them up the coast past Jenner-by-the-Sea in Sonoma County and then over through the redwoods into Mendocino. On the banks of the Eel River miles away from any paved roads, they had made love in the hot sun. She could still taste his sweat as if it had been yesterday.

"May the Lord have mercy," Mama Celeste sighed, "on my tired ass."

Striding along Market Street, Richard Rood was impatient to get to the Allen Hotel. Getting away from the cops had robbed him of energy; lassitude was doing a number on him. Recalling how the squad car had chased him through Stevenson Alley was enough to make him jittery all over again. The heat was on. Being in the streets wasn't safe anymore. That was how the police wanted it: let the outlaws rot indoors from inactivity.

Appraising the condition of his wardrobe, he was peeved. There was a rip in the shoulder seam of his patent leather jacket and a hole in the seat of his pants. The wind had shifted direction, affording Richard a whiff of himself. His suit was getting funky, simply because patent leather didn't breathe like other fabrics.

Rood didn't notice Mama Celeste until he practically trolled into her. He recognized her as the old lady he'd seen an hour ago. Shrinking back a step, he burred, "What the hell are you doing in my goddamn way? Can't you see I'm in a hurry?"

Mama Celeste stopped on a dime. She drank in Richard's appearance and saw a handsome man. His mouth was generous and intelligent. His eyes had red embers in them. His hands were aristocratic and feminine. His shoulders were wide and his hips svelte. Even the scar on his forehead was attractive.

"Where are you going?" she asked. "You're in a big rush, no?"

Agitated, Richard jiggled out a wide-toothed steel comb from his pants and worked his jheri curls with it. Grooming himself, fixing his hair, tamping it, pushing it into place, he glared at Mama. "What do you want to know that for? It ain't your business."

Mama Celeste took a second, longer look at him. He was a lot older than she'd originally guessed, maybe fifty. Her voice was steady when she said, "You never know. It might be."

"That's a load of foolishness if I've ever heard any," he said. "And excuse my French? But there are too many loudmouthed motherfuckers out here anyway and I ain't one of them." Richard bowed his head knowingly and pawed the sidewalk with his foot. Cars chugged up the street. A man and a woman with a shopping cart walked by. He said, "But that don't explain why you're speaking with me."

"Maybe you need a friend."

Friends: everybody had a few of them. Richard had dead friends. He had ex-friends and friends in prison that were serving life without parole. He sneezed and said, "I got a million friends. I got them coming out of my ass. More than I need."

"You don't look like you have any friends."

He smiled in anger, exposing three missing front teeth. "Oh, yeah? What else don't I have?"

"Money."

Richard whisked a hand over his damaged suit. "No kidding. I never have enough damn cabbage."

"Do you need some cash? I'll give it to you."

Mama Celeste was shorter than a tree stump. Richard couldn't pin down her nationality. Her accent was eastern European, high-pitched and nasal. But she looked black. She had the dark skin, the almond-shaped eyes, and the voluptuous lips of the motherland. She wanted to give him money? Richard Rood's jaw dropped an inch. She had to be raving. What a comedian. She ought to be on television. Stuffing the comb in his back pocket, he said, "Did I hear you right, sister? You want to give me money? I must be dreaming."

"You ain't."

"I ain't dreaming?"

"No."

"Then what is it that I'm doing?"

"Nothing. I just want to give you money."

"Then I must be going insane."

"You ain't doing that either."

"You the welfare office?"

"No."

"You the police?"

"No."

"You from the lottery?"

"No."

"You from another planet, you know, Pluto or something?"

"Nope."

"Then who the fuck are you?"

Richard was irate. The witch was setting him up to run a game on him. Toying with him. She was trying to outwit him and pull the wool over his eyes. If that's what she had planned, she had another thing coming. He said, "What's your scam?"

"My scam?"

"Yeah, the shit you're pulling here with me. You think I'm a mark or something? You trying to rob me?"

"No."

He ridiculed Mama Celeste. "You wearing a one-million-year-old army coat and you got on the funkiest damn shoes this side of the Mississippi River—Hunchback of Notre Dame wear that shit—and you want to give me money? You belong in the poor house. You styling like a homeless shelter. You don't have any money, no how."

A warm welcome, Mama Celeste didn't expect. A celebration of her presence wasn't necessary. But the denigration of her wardrobe was humiliating. There was no need to get personal. "You don't like my coat?" she shrugged. "Good for you. But let me tell you something. A coat is just a coat. It means nothing. And yes, I have money."

Richard mocked her. "You do not."

"Do too."

"You tripping." Richard couldn't take it any more—people were always talking big about their money. He called her bluff. "Prove it, girlfriend. Let's see it." That would show her who she was fucking with. She wanted to put some trick bag over on Richard Rood? No dice. She had to back up her play and show him what was what. There would be no half-stepping. No hoaxing. He waited and said, "Well? I ain't got all day."

Mama Celeste opened the shoebox and filched ten brand new one-hundred-dollar bills. She held the money in her palsying hands; the paper shimmered in the daylight. It trilled musically in the breeze, making a fanning sound. "Take it," she said. "It's a gift."

The proof was right in front of Richard Rood, but he didn't believe it. The money had to be bogus. It had to be a booby trap. It had to be an ambush. She was conning him. Thinking he was a dupe. Everybody was running a racket. Even this old dame had a gig she was hustling. He was too clever to fall for it. "Let me peruse that shit," he said.

Snatching the bills from Mama, Richard expertly ran his fingertips over the money. The paper was crisp. Good texture. The ink didn't smudge. Everything was in alignment and squared properly. The picture was solid. Ben Franklin looked like Ben Franklin. It wasn't a counterfeit. The cash was genuine. He grunted with reluctant approval. The money was tight. But what was she was doing with it? There was a ton of it in her box. And why was she giving some of it to him? She had nothing to gain by doing that. "It's the real McCoy," he admitted.

"Then keep it."

Richard cupped his ear. "Did I hear you right?"

"You did."

Giving money away to a total stranger made no sense to Richard Rood. It didn't compute. Nothing was for free. That was the way of the world. Whatever you wanted, you bought or absconded. If you couldn't do it, that was too bad—you had nobody to blame but yourself. A man without money wasn't alive. A man without the courage to steal what he needed was even less than that. Baffled, he asked, "What do you want from me?"

"Not a thing."

"That's malarkey. You gotta want something."

Mama was firm. "I don't want a damn thing from you."

"Then why are you doing this if you don't want nothing? You some kind of masochist?"

"Because God cares about you."

"God?" Richard was bamboozled. He jerked a thumb at his chest, maddened by what she'd said. "He cares about my butt?" He glanced over his shoulder to see if anyone was gaining on him. "That's bull pucky. He doesn't give a fuck about me. Never did."

"Yes, he does."

"Who says? I don't hear him saying shit. Never have. He doesn't even know who I am."

"I'm his messenger."

"You his what?"

Richard conjured up a likeness of the unsmiling Islamic brothers in suits and bow ties and fedoras who sold bean pies and peddled newspapers next to the BART entrance at Seventh and Market. Most of those dudes were ex-cons harder than nails. Richard was confused. People owed him money, beginning with that little white boy Stiv. The cops were on his tail. He was sick, maybe with a bug, maybe that hepatitis C, and this woman wanted to discuss religion? Bring up God? He couldn't cope. It was too deep for him. He said to Mama, "You ain't a Muslim, are you?"

Mama Celeste fit the lid back on the shoebox. The world was such a strange place. Everything was upside down. This man and her—she didn't even know his name—might never see each other again. At least one of them should profit from their meeting. "No, I'm not," she said. "I'm just doing what God instructed me to do."

"He told you to do this, to give me a bunch of hundreds? What did he do, call you up on the phone? Send you a fax?"

"No."

"But he wanted you to give me these here Franklins?"

God was in everything. He was in the office buildings, the trolley cars and in city hall. He was in the trees, in the flowers, in the clouds overhead. He was in newly minted cash. He was in the hearts of criminals too. Mama said, "He did. This money is his gospel."

"Why is he doing this?"

"Because you need it."

"How'd you know that?"

"Do you know anyone nowadays who doesn't need a thousand bucks?"

It dawned on Richard that he could take the shoebox from her. It would be a lark; the money was just sitting there. But he held himself back—it was torture to do that. Real bad. Impulse control had never been one of his virtues. "Where did you get this cash anyway? You a magician?"

"God gave it to me."

That shut his mouth. He couldn't argue with her about jack. Richard ogled the Franklins in his hand. Fingering the bills, he had no idea what he'd done to deserve them. Not a damn thing. He blinked steadily at Mama Celeste and said, "Well, hey, yeah, uh, thanks, sister."

"You're welcome."

Richard Rood had a peek at Market Street. The cars in the road were thinning. No cops were in the vicinity. He had to press on. He put the cash in his wallet and without uttering another word to Mama Celeste, resumed his safari to the Allen Hotel.

NINE

MARKET STREET HOSTED the Saint Patrick's Day parade and the Gay Pride celebrations in the Civic Center. Hundreds of thousands of tourists came from all over the world to witness these events. The visitors purchased postcards to send back home. They bought souvenir T-shirts from street side vendors. They squandered wheelbarrows of money in restaurants. None of them ever stayed at the Allen Hotel.

It was how Jeeter Roche wanted it—no unwanted intruders were welcome in his castle. Squatting on the chipped marble staircase in the hotel's portico, he cleaned the wax from his ears with a wooden matchstick. Jeeter's leisure suit jacket sleeves were tied frat-boy style over his brawny shoulders. His feet were squeezed into a pair of spanking new Tony Lama cowboy boots. A purple cyst reigned over his brow like an all-knowing third eye.

Sitting at his side with a small hill of bills by her feet was Chiclet. Her imitation Dior dress was hiked up above her tanned thighs. The silver bracelets on her wiry arms jangled as she counted the week's tally. The money was from the tenants on all five floors, a grand total of $13,600. Eight hundred of it was earmarked for Jeeter.

The flies on the walls stirred at the sound of Jeeter's tinny voice. He quarreled, "Eight hundred dollars? That's all I get? That is fucking chump change. It's preposterous. How am I supposed to deal with that shit? It simply isn't enough. Speaking of the devil, did Stiv Wilkins pay his rent yet?"

Chiclet chewed on a pencil. Insulated within the Valium's labyrinthine depths, Jeeter and the rest of the city seemed far off. Her head was as weightless as a feather. She was in an orbit of spatial distortion. Her brain was ten miles from her feet. She said, "No, he hasn't."

"He's late? Again?" Jeeter was confounded. "That bum. He's gone too far with it. We're in a codependent relationship with him."

"Yeah, he's blowing it. Stiv don't have much money."

"Too bad for us. Did he even pay up from last week? He said he was going to."

Chiclet leafed through the pages of her receipt book. "No."

"Fucking empty promises. It's unbelievable. That's the fifth time this year, damn him."

Jeeter's mouth soured into a moon of discontent. Difficult tenants were plain evil and Stiv Wilkins was no exception to the rule. Maybe he'd set Stiv's room on fire, a time-honored tradition at the Allen for dealing with fractious renters. Burn the fucker right out of the hotel. Jeeter had read Tolstoy, and had entertained pacifism. In his business, it wasn't practical. He said, "We'll call my lawyer over there on Montgomery Street and get a process server out here to hit Stiv with a three day notice for failure to pay, okay?"

"Okay."

"I want that clod out of my hair. He's robbing us. We need to evict the two-bit asshole. Then we can say sayonara to Stiv Wilkins, thank God."

"If that's what you want."

Jeeter was prickly. "What, you got any objections?"

Careful with her reply, Chiclet said, "Stiv's not that bad."

"The fuck he ain't. You're losing money on him, too, you know."

Safely concealed behind the staircase, Stiv heard everything Jeeter Roche said. The threat of eviction didn't come as a shock, and he wasn't daunted by it. The landlord had disliked him from the day they'd met. In kind, Stiv had never trusted him. The ex-con dressed horribly. How could you trust someone who wore polyester flares belted above the waistline? The answer was simple. You didn't. It would be a cold day in hell before the dork ever saw a nickel from him. Stiv sneaked away without being seen and hastened upstairs to call his social worker.

In compliance with the terms of his probation—the collateral damage from the six months spent in jail—Stiv was supposed to telephone Norbert Deflass every day. This was a cinch and it was easier than reporting in person. He didn't have to deal with the cops. There were no pee tests. He didn't have to shave or dress up if he didn't want to. Shoving two quarters into the pay phone on the fourth floor, he dialed the Shotwell Street mental health clinic.

Norbert answered the telephone on the tenth ring. A boom box was howling in the background. "Extension twenty. Deflass here. Who's this?"

"Uh, it's me, Stiv Wilkins."

The social worker radiated joie de vivre. "Stiv, babe. What's up? Has it been twenty-four hours already?"

"Yeah, that's why I'm calling."

"So, what's cooking?"

Stiv was discreet. "Nothing."

"Nothing? Are you sure? Something's got to be going down. Talk to me, baby."

Deflass was a professional—he'd suck your biography out of you like a vacuum cleaner—but Stiv wasn't going to talk about his hallucinations. Deflass would demand that he turn himself into the psych unit at General Hospital on Potrero Street. The doctors would hold him for seventy-two hours and dose him with Prolixin, a stronger cousin of Haldol. He'd spend his waking hours in the day room drawing with crayons on paper. The nights would be spent listening to the other patients in the ward talk in their sleep.

Stiv said, "Everything's cool, really. No problems."

"How are your wife and son?"

Stiv didn't know where they were. Maybe they were at the food stamp office. He said, "They're cool."

"The boy getting big?"

The kid had been born fat. Stiv said, "Yeah."

"Have you named him yet?"

"No."

"Your wife, you getting along with her?"

Alone in the hallway, Stiv lit a cigarette before answering the question. A finger of smoke circled his quiff. He said, "Yeah."

"What about you then?"

The social worker was talking about Stiv's least favorite subject. He waffled. "Who, me?"

"Yeah, you."

"I'm fine."

Honing in, Deflass said, "Are you doing the Haldol like I told you to?"

Talking about the medication you were on wasn't fun. You might as well admit you were a chicken hawk in a kindergarten classroom or a peeping tom at the neighbor's window. Stiv was ashamed and secretive about taking Haldol. He said, "No, I ain't. I stopped."

Trumpeting his displeasure, Deflass cut in. "The prescription ran out?"

"No."

"What?"

"I was getting sick of it. The stuff is nauseating, dude."

"So?"

"The shit is vicious. I don't like it. It gives me dry mouth. I have trouble walking. I shuffle."

Deflass paid no heed to Stiv's complaints. "Call up the pharmacy and order more. Do it now, Stiv. You like hallucinating? You like seeing ghosts?"

"Nah, it's a drag."

"If you don't take the Haldol, they'll get worse."

"Uh huh."

"How old are you?"

Stiv loathed his age. "I'm twenty-five, older than the fucking hills."

There was an acute silence at the other end of the line. Then, "You're a parent now, Stiv. You have to stop thinking about yourself all the time. There are other people you're responsible for."

"Don't bug me with that, Deflass. I'm living with them, you ain't."

"You need to clean up your act. Do you want to remain mentally ill for the rest of your life?"

"I ain't ill. You're the one saying that, not me. If I was sick, don't you think I'd be the first to know it, hah?"

"Then what are you gonna do?"

"I don't know."

"You're a musician, aren't you? You sing, yeah?"

The cops had shut down his band's first gig in the city, the same night they came in from Portland. Stiv had sung one number before he was unplugged. The police confiscated the sound system. Stiv got into a fight in the bathroom with two jocks and walked away from it with a black eye. He said, "Not these days."

Deflass grunted. "So let's get smart. You need to take the pills as prescribed. Seriously, I've got to insist on the Haldol. You have to get back on it. We can lower the dosage and see if that works better for you."

Stiv was stubborn. "I don't want to. It makes me feel real fucking bad. Like I'm gonna cut my throat or something."

"Tough shit. You get some today because if you're not on medication, that gives me cause to say you're violating probation. You don't want that to happen, do you?" A hideous wall of electronic dissonance smothered Deflass's voice. He faded and then came back. "Stiv? I've got another call coming in. Get to me later about this."

"When?"

"I just told you. Later. Okay?"

"Okay."

"Ciao."

What an asshole, Stiv thought.

65

Stiv floated on a cloud of tobacco smoke down the hall to his room. He opened the door and was displeased to find the place dark and stuffy. He hoisted the venetian blinds and a bar of pissy sunlight crept in. There was a note for him in Sharona's handwriting on the sink counter. He picked it up and read her discursive scrawl—she and the baby were down at the laundromat. They'd be back in a couple of hours.

He sat at the table with the note in his hand. No curtains hung from the window. No pictures decorated the walls. There was no rug on the linoleum floor. The hotel room had the flavor of a minimum-security penal institution. He tuned the portable radio in to the NPR news. A female reporter with a horsey voice was chattering about the Brinks fiasco, announcing that millions of unmarked dollars had been stolen.

Finished with his cigarette, he extinguished it in the palm of his hand. The news reporter had moved on to international events and was talking about American troops fighting guerrillas in the Philippines. Stiv lowered the volume to an unintelligible garble when she started to recite the day's body count. A second later there was a knock on the door. He jumped up and walked over to the peephole. He looked in it and saw a female in the hall. He said, "Who the hell is it? I'm busy."

"Stiv? Are you there?"

"Who is this?"

"It's me, Chiclet."

He shut his eyes and pursed his lips. This was not good. Her, he didn't need. Not now or next year. The facts were the facts: an unannounced visit from Chiclet Dupont was an invitation into quicksand. She probably wanted the rent money. It was hell. Stiv glanced at Sharona's note, felt a surge of guilt, and shouted through the door, "What do you want? I'm in the middle of something very important in here."

"We need to speak. It's urgent."

"About what?"

"Let me in and I'll explain."

His first impulse was, no thank you. Chiclet was a passel of hassles. On the other hand, as she was the landlord's wife, he had to stay on her good side and make sure that he didn't offend her. It was a chess game and he had to think fast. "The door's open," he said. "Come on in."

In preened Chiclet. She brushed past him in a puff of cheap perfume. Her unfettered cleavage was outlined against the phony Dior. Her toenails were painted scarlet red. Her ivory feet were encased in open-toed sandals and she wore a twenty-four-carat gold chain around her right ankle. Her seasick brown eyes were unreadable.

She seated herself in the room's sole chair, a rocker that Stiv had rescued from a garbage Dumpster. Sucking on a Marlboro Light, Chiclet tapped the cigarette. A four-inch ash landed on Stiv's unpolished engineer boots. Projecting disdain, she said, "You're fucking up again."

His heart stopped beating for a pulse. "How so?"

"A quandary is coming at you."

A neighbor's laughter seeped through the paper-thin walls. Stiv didn't know what a quandary was. It sounded like a late model sports car. Maybe it was a nuclear missile. Possibly it was a new detergent, or a lethal germ. He said, as if his ignorance were somebody else's fault, "What about it?"

Needing to occupy her hands, Chiclet picked up a kapok pillow and held it to her nose. It stank of Walgreens drugstore brand shampoo. She said, "Jeeter don't like you."

Stiv made as if he didn't know what she was referring to. "He doesn't?"

"Nope."

"How come?"

"You owe him rent."

Stiv grinned, a corner of his mouth turning brittle. "Too damn bad."

Chiclet put the pillow in her lap and drilled him with a hot glance. "But I like you." She raised one manicured eyebrow. Valium made her horny, a little unhinged, and slightly off-course. Jeeter was in the drug room and wouldn't care if she were gone for a few minutes. All he was concerned about was money and his books. Time flew when you were married to Jeeter Roche. One day turned into a week and suddenly, two months was yesterday. Having sex with Jeeter went even quicker. He rarely lasted more than a New York minute. His quickness had forced Chiclet to ask herself, where had all the good times gone?

"Stiv?"

"Yeah, baby?"

"You're sweet," she chimed. "Give me a kiss."

He clasped her hand and leaned into her face. Chiclet's skin was chalky with Johnson's baby powder. He swept her mouth with his puckered lips, tasting the Valium's tang as her sandpapery tongue telescoped between his teeth. A sudden heat rushed into his groin, and he sprang an erection that was palpable through his worn out black Dickies. Hoping to hide it, he turned sideways.

The tension between the two of them was a frozen rope that stretched from his mouth to her mouth. Looking at Chiclet, Stiv didn't know what he was feeling. Excitement. Dread. It was a cocktail of lust and repulsion. Her sweet and sour breath was wet on his neck. She had his hand trapped between her knees. Feeling his cock against her leg, she guided Stiv's fingers under her dress.

"I want you to kneel, Stiv."

He didn't like the sound of it. "What for?" he balked. "You know I don't do that sort of thing."

"C'mon."

Stiv was reluctant. "You ain't messing with me, are you?"

"No, no, I'm not."

Ever the pragmatist, he demanded, "What's in it for me?"

Chiclet giggled. "You'll see."

He submitted. "If you say so."

Sliding onto his knees, he crouched between her legs. Her thighs were shapely and covered with whitened down. To his astonishment, she wasn't wearing any underwear. Not even a bikini thong. Her auburn pubic hair had been shaved into a neat triangle and smelled fruity.

Chiclet issued a throaty laugh. "Lick me."

Stiv figured, why not? Taking a gulp of air, he tongued her slit. She was pleased by his initiative. "Yeah, that's it."

He gagged on his spit. His lungs had no oxygen, and breathing was impossible. Suffocation was imminent. There were worse ways to die, but not so many that he could think of. He saw the headlines in tomorrow's newspaper—man expires mysteriously in woman's bush—autopsy shows nothing. Stiv urged himself to remain calm. Getting Chiclet off would be easy, a piece of cake. His tongue was singing inside her as if it were a violin. But something went awry. A salty glob adhered itself to his lips; his tongue and mouth were on fire from the discharge. He lifted his head and said, "What the fuck is that shit?"

Chiclet's remorse was captured in a stoned out contralto. "Oh, that?" There was no point in hiding the truth. There was no way to spare Stiv's dignity. She said, "Yeah, well, Jeeter and me? We fucked earlier this morning and I haven't had a chance to shower off yet. Bummer, huh?"

Stiv's face was instantly drained of color. Shellacked with Jeeter's seed, his lips burned. Chiclet had stabbed him in the back and it put Stiv in touch with all the other times he'd been double-crossed. Like when he'd failed kindergarten because the teacher said he didn't understand the difference between good and bad. Or how he'd taken a felony assault charge on a cop for a friend who let him take the blame. But this was worse than all that. This was a disaster. Clumsily getting to his feet, he cursed, "Fuck, you could've warned me or something."

Chiclet had a yank at her tacky dress and said, "You look bad. You aren't gonna barf, are you?"

He gestured at her, moving his arms, but couldn't speak. Bells tolled in his ears. His intestines churned with a life of their own. The floor was moving under his feet. He slumped forward and collapsed, walloping his forehead on the chair. Dust balls moiled around his face. The last thing Stiv saw before he blacked out was the ghost of José Reyna climbing in the window.

José's freshly washed hair was as glossy as a raven's wing. His handsome profile exuded health. His expression was agreeable, his eyes were clear, and his skin was fair. Several pistols were tucked into the purple and red wool sash girding his waist. His silver and bronze spurs jingled as he walked.

Another man in the regalia of a *mexicano* cowboy, suede chaps and a buckskin jacket with silver buttons, accompanied the outlaw. It was his cousin, a teenager known to the police as Two-Fingered Tom. Two-Fingered was in a foul mood and bickered with José. Soon they'd have to sneak into San Francisco to pull off a robbery, crossing the bay from Oakland in a canoe built by Ohlone Indian mixed-bloods. They needed the cash, but Two-Fingered wasn't looking forward to the excursion. San Francisco had too many gringos and made him antsy. Like his *primo*, he never liked standing in one place for too long.

"*Hijo de la gran puta*, what are we doing?" he railed. "*Los puercos* are after us and when they find our asses, they're gonna wipe us out. So you snuffed those dudes who killed your woman. You did what you had to do. But now what?" He flourished the mutilated hand that had earned him the infamous nickname. "We're in deep shit, *vato*."

José's emotions boiled to the surface, but he refrained from talking. He tried to remember his wife. What she looked like before she was raped and slain by a pack of gringo gold miners. He had already tracked down fifteen members of the mob that had murdered her. There were moments when José could hardly believe he'd just turned twenty-one years old.

Hunting his wife's killers with the instincts of a bloodhound, José had found the last two at a camp fifty miles outside of Marysville. The twosome was tending a small campfire under a weeping willow tree in a creek bottom. The air was hot and somnolent; flies and mosquitoes afflicted their corralled ponies. The first gringo was short and roly-poly with a ginger beard and a red face. His partner was reedy and thin with a sallow mug. They were sharing an earthenware jug of moonshine.

Dismounting from his horse and tying it to a copse of datura in a ravine, José took out a knife with a deer bone handle. He stuck it between his teeth and belly-crawled through the creek's low-lying brush. He waited until his prey was asleep and then cut the roly-poly man's throat, severing his vocal cords, letting him choke in his own blood. Stripping his partner naked and staking him out on the sandy ground, José chopped off his fingers and toes one by one before shooting him five times in the mouth.

Stiv came out of the fugue as the ghosts of José Reyna and Two-Fingered Tom dissolved into nothingness. Their faces and voices, and then their clothes, boots, and weapons atomized. He raised his head and moved his feet. No bones were broken. He twisted his neck: it still worked. His arms and legs were numb, disconnected from the rest of him. He was alone and the room was spinning in circles.

He lay there for a couple of minutes, listening to his heart. It was banging against his rib cage with the fury of a wild animal. Woozily, he clambered to his feet and jetted out the door into the hall. It was quiet; he could hear his own asthmatic breathing. He gadded downstairs into the lobby and then outside.

A bunch of yellow-eyed black starlings were sunning themselves on a Market Street fence. Stiv saw an audience and jived the birds as if they were his comrades. He put his hands in his motorcycle jacket, and said, "Listen, guys. I need money. I need lots of money to get the fuck away from this place."

Hearing his trebly voice, the starlings flew off in a panic. Feeling rejected—even the birds couldn't handle him—Stiv stared hard at the street. The traffic was backed up for three blocks to the red light on Van Ness Avenue because a truck had broken down in the road. Stiv wiped a runny nose with the back of his hand and reckoned on what he had. It didn't amount to much. Fifty dollars in his wallet, and only a few hours left to pay the rent and Richard Rood.

TEN

CHICLET DUG HER FINGERNAILS into the hallway banister and held on for dear life. The Valium was rushing over her in tidal waves, each one bigger than its predecessor. Maybe she needed to do some crystal meth to get her biorhythms in balance. A cold Budweiser would be nice too—anything to kill the taste of the Allen Hotel in her mouth. She reached in her Ralph Lauren purse for the drug room keys and couldn't find them. Her heart pounced into her throat: Jeeter would massacre her if she ever lost them.

Her ears pricked up when she heard footsteps on the carpeted staircase, and she waited to see who it was. But her curiosity flagged as the footfall grew nearer. God help her if it was Jeeter. She didn't have the strength to contend with him right now. It was impossible to talk to the lummox when she was loaded. He was so pushy, do this and do that, she couldn't hold her own with him around.

Cresting the fifth floor landing, Sharona let the laundry bag fall at her feet. Dressed in tight black denim Wrangler jeans, a black turtleneck sweater, and gold hoop earrings, she had on black lipstick and black loafers. A pair of zircon-encrusted sunglasses nested in her platinum blonde bouffant. She shifted the baby in her arms and saw Chiclet in the hallway's shadows.

The landlord's doper wife looked like something the cat had dragged in. Chiclet's dress was unzipped down the back. Her eyes were huge and bloodshot. One of her sandals was missing a buckle. Her hair was a haystack, sticking out in all directions. Cardinal red lipstick was smudged on her left cheek. A sterling silver earring dangled from her left ear. Sharona played it cool and picked up the laundry bag and started toward her room.

Chiclet cozied up to her. "Hey, wait a minute."

Sharona was preoccupied with a dozen things that had to be done. The baby was hungry and wanted nursing. The garbage had to be taken out. She had to sew a torn bra strap. The brat's milk bottles needed boiling. Chiclet's eyes were eating her alive. Sharona couldn't remember the last time she'd seen that much loneliness in one person. The woman was an asteroid from outer space.

"What do you want?" Sharona asked.

Chiclet was too stoned to be diplomatic. "My husband's gonna evict you and Stiv for not paying the rent."

It wasn't news to Sharona. Jeeter Roche was always threatening to put them in the street. She stuck her chin out and harpooned Chiclet with a fleer. "So the fuck what?"

Because she had made love with Stiv, Chiclet felt connected to Sharona. They had shared a man and this bound them together. She knew the feeling was unrequited but didn't care. She touched the younger woman's arm. "Honey, I didn't mean to be brusque. I'm just trying to help you."

Gratitude wasn't in Sharona's vocabulary. Not when she was paying $170 a week at the Allen. The toilets in the hall overflowed every time you turned on the sink in your room. There were power outages daily. She manufactured a smile from equal parts of anger and sarcasm. "Thanks for the tip. That's real nice of you. Now if you'll excuse me, I've got to change the baby's diapers. I think he just took a dump."

Dropping the clothes on the bed in the room, Sharona chucked the brat in a swaddle of blankets and peeled off his soiled nappies. His poop was an ochre-hued puree, a vivid contrast to his ivory-colored skin. Using the premoistened wipes that Stiv had shoplifted the day before from a Rite-Aid drugstore, Sharona swabbed the boy's tush. Plump legs churning, he goggled at her with round eyes. "What did you do?" she said.

Booboo scowled. "Ga-ga."

"Did you go ga-ga in your nappies?"

He responded with a sustained belch and reached for her breasts. Every time Booboo went poo-poo, it reminded him that he was hungry. Sharona tucked a new diaper around his butt, pulled up her sweater, and unfastened her nursing bra. Having a baby had increased her coordination and manual dexterity. She had learned to do two things at the same time.

"You want some titty?"

Her breast was delicate with blue and red capillaries. The nipple was marble-hard and the areola was dark brown. Booboo regarded it with awe. Wheeling her tit like she was piloting a ship into port, Sharona brought his mouth to it.

As he suckled, her eyes grew heavy lidded. The sun in the window warmed her face. September's heat was welcome after August's coldness, but the morning's fog had declared a hint of winter was in the air.

A year ago she'd been single and didn't even know who Stiv Wilkins was. Then she got in a car wreck with two boys and another girl in a '67 Mustang near the Devil's Slide, north of Half Moon Bay in San Mateo County. The boy at the wheel had been drinking and broadsided a Greyhound charter bus coming into the city.

Ejected from the back seat during the impact, Sharona was propelled onto the asphalt. Because she was in the path of oncoming traffic, she was run over by a VW Passat. An ambulance came a few minutes later and she was scraped off the pavement. Blood was rushing from her mouth, nose, eyes, and ears. Wanting to vomit, she conked out cold.

She woke up in the critical ward at Seton Medical Center in Daly City. Leaking blood from one ear onto the gurney, she passed out again. She regained consciousness in the intensive care unit the next day. A doctor was leaning over her gurney. He was young, unshaven and bored. He held out three fingers. "How many?" he asked.

She croaked, "Two."

He held up four fingers. "Now how many?"

"Three."

"Can you tell me the name of the president of the United States?"

"I don't know it."

"What year did the Americans land on the moon?"

"Huh?"

"It was 1969. Well, my dear," he said. "You've had a major concussion."

"What about my friends?"

The doctor was honest. "They died."

There was a swelling behind her right ear and she was hospitalized for seven days. The Mustang's driver made a cameo appearance in a dream on the fourth night. His face was bloody and he was missing an arm. Unable to converse, he mimed with his remaining hand. He had three basic questions. One, where was he? Two, why was he alone? Three, would the darkness ever end? The nurse's station backlighted his near-translucent body. He waved the stump of his missing arm; his charred eyes begged her to answer his questions. Sharona opened her mouth to comfort him, but nothing came out.

After leaving the hospital, Sharona met Stiv at a friend's party and he invited her back to his room. Against her better judgment, they had sex. Looking back, she had to admit that it had been her idea.

Upon discovering she was pregnant, Sharona set up a schedule for prenatal classes and got indigent Medi-Cal insurance to cover the maternity costs. Stiv, not surprisingly, had been missing in action. During her second and third trimesters, he sent her postcards from jail, saying he was doing fine.

Sharona regarded the clock. It was two in the afternoon. Christ only knew where Stiv was. It was best not to think about it. There were times when she looked in his limpid eyes and didn't know who he was. Or what country he was from. You got the feeling he didn't know either. With the baby at her breast, she turned on the radio—the broadcast was about the Brinks job. A representative for the company vowed the thieves would suffer the full penalty of the law. Kissing the top of her child's fuzzy dome, Sharona said to him, "Shit, we need some money, don't we, sugar bear?"

Booboo pried his lips off her tit and beamed a toothless smile at his mother. "Ga-ga."

When the hour struck three, Richard Rood materialized at the entrance of Jeeter Roche's Stevenson Alley residence. The scar on his forehead ached as it always did when the weather was foggy. He gave the sky a withering look. The sun was pissing about behind a mackerel cloud. The walk up Market Street had been a royal pain. The high point had been meeting Mama Celeste. But the money she gave him didn't change anything. The cop had chumped him. His clothes were trashed. The flu was killing him. Stiv Wilkins was going to pay for all that.

He gave the security door a shove and it opened. A blast of Pine-Sol all-purpose cleaning liquid flayed his skin as he crossed the threshold. Richard Rood cursed and went through the vestibule and repaired up the staircase.

All the while questioning his own sanity, he stomped up four long flights of stairs. Some of the slats were missing, causing him to stub his toe. The building was a furnace. It was the coal room in Hades. It was the devil's own home. Must have been five hundred degrees in there. Richard was perspiring as if he had malaria. People were screaming and babies were hollering and radios were blasting music. Water gurgled in the plumbing under the floor. A mockingbird was singing on a fire escape. Tearing off his jacket, he wrapped the garment around his head in a turban. He gained the fifth floor landing and pussyfooted it through the stifling hallway.

The third door on the left opened and a young woman came out of a smoke-filled room. She paused in the doorway to light a clove cigarette. Her petite feet were clad in Moroccan sandals. Her black silk bathrobe was loose around her waist. Her hair was tied back with a turquoise-blue linen ribbon. Her face was slathered in Revlon cold cream.

Richard's visage hardened into basalt. The girl was Jeeter Roche's old lady. He gave her the once-over from head to foot. She was coltish and high as a kite. Must be having a bad day. He called out to her in a desultory whine overlaid with absolute menace. "Hey, beauty queen, I need a word with you."

Instantly recognizing his basso voice, Chiclet jumped out of her skin. Jeeter had talked often enough about the guy. He'd warned her more than once: "If this ugly black motherfucker ever comes here looking for me, it means you've just gone to someplace that's worse than hell. Much worse. He's psycho. He's short and talks like a frog. Dresses like a freak. You watch your ass around him."

Swaggering over to her, Richard Rood stood at arm's length and licked his lips to see if he could get a reaction. When Chiclet didn't take the bait, he stated his quest. He was succinct. He was polite. He didn't mince words. He was explicit. "Listen, baby cakes, I'm looking for your husband, that Jeeter Roche dude. He knows somebody I have to get next to."

Chiclet was exquisitely loaded, the right combination of vertigo and weightlessness. She didn't give a rat's ass about Richard's needs. She exhaled a perfectly executed smoke ring, saying, "Jeeter? He ain't here."

Richard was dubious. "Oh, yeah? Where is he? I'm on urgent business."

"He's out taking care of things. What do you want?"

"I have to talk with him about some information. Vital shit."

Chiclet's unfriendly eyes were two red holes in the white cold cream. "About what?" she said.

Richard corrected her. "It ain't what, but who. I'm looking for Stiv Wilkins. You know that punk?"

"Nope."

Richard nodded. "C'mon, kitty-cat, be honest with me. I understand you doing Stiv."

Chiclet looked at him as if he were a eunuch. "That ain't so."

"I hear otherwise," Richard said. "People say you fuck him on the sly."

She dared him to refute her. "People lie, don't they?"

He was philosophical. "For sure, but all you have to do is tell me where I can find this Stiv Wilkins."

"I don't know who he is."

"Please don't say that again, sugar cube. It upsets me." Spicing his request with the only Italian word he knew, Richard said, "The sooner you help me find him, the happier you and me will be. *Capiche?*"

A vein throbbed on Chiclet's temple and she had an inkling of danger. Maybe it was how the dude was talking. Maybe it was how he looked at her. Maybe it was the suit he wore. Jeeter wouldn't have approved of it. Where she came from in the East Bay, out in suburban Concord, there weren't too many guys that dressed like Richard Rood. She snuffled, "I can't help you, man, okay?"

Richard opened his mouth in a sick smile, displaying a battlefield of unfinished dental work. His breath was harsh and vinegary, potent enough to ream the hair off a dog. He raised a hand; ten-carat gold rings glimmered on every finger. He said, "You can't? That's a goddamn shame. Why don't we just go on inside and discuss it then?"

His hollow voice broached no protest. Doing a three-sixty, Chiclet sidled into the apartment. Following her, Richard inspected the place with a professional eye. The dining area contained a vintage formica-top table with three matching chairs. A door opened to a bedroom; a king-sized futon bed and a rectangular olive-green macramé carpet occupied the floor space. The sheets on the bed were paisley flannel. A pile of unwashed clothes guarded one corner. The open closet door revealed a battalion of shoes. The kitchen was in the other direction by the bathroom. A Nautilus weight machine was in the hall. Richard saw nothing that he liked and expressed his contempt by saying, "Jeeter got any toot here? Anything good?"

Chiclet was offended by his intrusive tone. "We ain't got any."

"Don't give me that baloney. He's slanging the shit. He's got to have some around. Something recreational. Just a little toot, you know?"

"We don't do business at home."

"You don't? Pardon me. Where do you do it then?"

"The Allen Hotel."

Richard smirked. "That a fact?" He turned his attention to Chiclet and objectified her with the same kind of heartbreaking coldness that he had used on the furniture. She had bad skin under all that cream. Dyed punk rock hair. Interesting bathrobe. Her eyes weren't close set together. She wasn't too ugly. He walked around the living room with his chin in his hand and dawdled by the window. "So you don't know Stiv, huh? I thought everyone damn well did. The man is contagious."

Chiclet reaffirmed her ignorance. "I ain't acquainted with him."

"Well, maybe you is and maybe you ain't." Richard cracked his knuckles and bruised her with a vampirish stare. It was an embittered gaze that x-rayed her inner nature and saw a vacancy sign. He said in an off-handed manner, "I got a special request."

She wasn't keen to hear it and affected a yawn. "You do?"

"I certainly do," Richard said. "I want you to take off that bathrobe you got on."

His demand sounded like it came from Mars. From an interplanetary source that was millions of miles away. Maintaining her composure, Chiclet stalled for time by killing the cigarette in an ashtray. Gongs were clashing in her head. Nausea liquefied in her stomach, and her hands were clammy. There was no doubt about it: the heel was going to have a go at her ass. She gauged the distance between him and her and glanced around the room for a weapon. A letter opener on the sink counter fit the bill, but Richard Rood saw what she was looking at and put it in the sink.

"Don't be shy," he beseeched her. "I ain't got all day."

"Are you serious?"

"Like a toothache, girl."

There was no way out. She'd have to jump from the window to get away from him. The cops would find her on the sidewalk with her head cracked open. Nobody would blame Richard Rood. The coroner would trace all that Valium in her and call her death a fluke.

Unbelting the robe, she shrugged the garment from her shoulders and it fell to the rug.

Richard Rood nodded approvingly. This was the first time that he'd ever seen a naked woman outside of a strip joint and the chick wasn't half terrible. She had a swan's neck, perky breasts with large nipples, and a filigreed silver chain around her tummy. He admired the muscular tone of her legs. He also appreciated her bush. It was neatly shaven, a perfect pyramid. Highly stylized, like his red suit. Exactly how he liked things. "Okay, good," he said. "That's all. Thank you."

The adrenaline, cortisol, and other stress hormones in Chiclet's bloodstream had killed the tranquilizing effects of the Valium. She was as sober as the day she'd been born. Crossing her arms over her breasts, she spat, "What do you mean, thank you? You ain't gonna tie me up?"

"Nah."

"You're not going to beat me?"

"No, gorgeous, I ain't."

"You ain't going to fuck me?"

"No. Pipe down. No need to get all excited."

"Don't get excited? Fuck off, you."

Richard was swift to say, "Shit, girlfriend, I'm gay. If I want to hump someone, it sure won't be you or any other woman. Not in this lifetime or in the next one. I definitely am not into that shit. I was just giving you a look-see, learning about this here female anatomy thing."

The strains of "Stormy Monday Blues" by Bobby Blue Bland insinuated themselves through the walls from a neighbor's phonograph. The scratches on the ancient vinyl were as loud as the music itself. Done with his business, Richard Rood shambled to the door and swung it open. The unoiled hinges squeaked in agony. His broad shoulders grazed both sides of the doorframe as he turned to give Chiclet a penetrating glance. A glance that said he was taking a hunk of her soul with him.

"You tell Jeeter I came by," he said evenly. "Tell him that I want to talk."

ELEVEN

I N JULY 1916 a bomb went off at a War Preparedness Day parade on Market Street. The procession had just gotten underway at the Embarcadero when the explosion ripped out a chunk of the Southern Pacific Building at the corner of Market and Steuart, injuring nearby spectators. Two local union men, Tom Mooney and Warren K. Billings, were arrested for the crime. Both claimed innocence during their trial.

The jury found them guilty and they were sent to prison. Then, after twenty-three years of confinement, the governor of California, a man named Culbert Olsen, pardoned Billings and Mooney. Forty thousand people attended a welcome home rally for Tom Mooney at the Civic Center. He died three years later at Saint Luke's Hospital in the Mission district following surgery.

At Folsom State Prison, where Warren Billings served his sentence, there was a mural version of *The Last Supper* in the church chapel. A convict artist had used Billings's face as a model for one of the twelve apostles seated at the table with Christ. When Billings got out of the joint, he became a watch repairman and opened a shop on Market Street.

Walking up Jones Street, Mama Celeste was hungry and made a straight line to Saint Anthony Dining Room. The queue into the soup kitchen was three blocks long, winding over to Golden Gate Avenue and then down onto Leavenworth Street.

Saint Anthony was a Catholic charity, the flagship in the city's fleet of soup kitchens. Operated by priests in a subterranean cafeteria next to an abandoned bank, it fed thousands of indigents daily.

Joining the very end of the line, Mama Celeste jiggled up and down on one foot. Her bladder was full, a result of the tea she'd been drinking. Thinking about going to the bathroom was absurd. How fast folks were getting in line behind her, she'd lose her spot if she went somewhere to relieve herself. Mama had to make a choice. Should she go find a place to take a leak or stay where she was? She hadn't had a bite to eat since dawn. Her empty stomach settled the issue and she thought no more about it.

Mama cast a side-glance at a clock in a storefront window. It was three forty-five. She did a rough head count—two thousand people were ahead of her in the queue. The soup kitchen clientele were mostly men and a few females, all lugging suitcases and rucksacks and pillowcases stuffed with their possessions. Some had dogs. Others had cats. A few had shopping carts.

The sun, tangoing in and out of the fog, flung a shadow over the street. Pigeons were squatting on a parked police van's roof. A hooker in torn nylons was doing her makeup in the window of a Mercury station wagon up on four cinder blocks. A gaggle of black kids in knit caps and goose down parkas was at the corner. One kid reached in his pocket and a Smith and Wesson revolver, an itty-bitty nickel-plated .32 caliber gat, fell out and hit the sidewalk with a clatter.

Mama tucked the shoebox under her coat and stripped a gummy copy of the *San Francisco Chronicle* off the ground. The lead article on the newspaper's front page was about the Brinks robbery. There was a photograph of the Brinks truck after the crash. The vehicle lay on its side, resembling a wounded buffalo.

An hour later Mama was ushered through the soup kitchen's doors and herded down a concrete loading ramp by a burly security guard with a flashlight. The tunnel was moldy and unlit and she had a premonition of catastrophe. What her foreboding was about, she didn't know.

A brown-robed priest with a tonsured hairdo escorted Mama into the immense dining room. A sea of badly dressed people ate at a hundred rough-hewn pinewood picnic tables. Thanking the friar for the personal touch, Mama said, "Bless you, father. I'm glad to be here."

"You're welcome, my daughter," the priest replied. "This is the oasis of the Tenderloin. You come often?"

"All the time, ever since my husband died."

"We're glad to have you. Consider us your home away from home."

Glomming a tray from a stack, Mama set the shoebox on it, and then collected a spoon, fork, and knife. A sanguine ex-con in a hair net gave her a bowl of instant oatmeal, a plateful of powdered eggs, orange slices, and a cup of instant coffee. The quartered orange slices scintillated in the cafeteria's fluorescent lighting; the eggs were steaming, and the oatmeal was gelatinous.

Mama made herself cozy at a table laden with cartons of tomato juice, loaves of day-old white bread, baskets of apples, ketchup bottles, and saltshakers, and began to chow down. Spooning oatmeal in her gob, she peeked over the cereal bowl's rim at the rest of the room.

The soup kitchen's decor wasn't anything to write home about. The concrete walls were painted prison pea green. The floor was fatigued linoleum tiling. There was a full-color oil portrait of Jesus Christ in his prime on the door. Security guards in windbreakers roamed the aisles just in case a client went crazy. Pushed around by the cops, cheated out of their welfare checks by liquor store cashiers, and unable to stay dry because of the fog and rain, people fresh off the street were testy.

Eating and reading at another table was Jeeter Roche. The Allen Hotel's manager was alone and modestly clothed in a puce-colored goose down vest and oversized Phat Farm jeans. A paperback, the novel *Gabriela, Clove, and Cinnamon* by the Brazilian writer Jorge

Amado, was propped against a tub of margarine. Engrossed in the story, Jeeter forked powdered eggs into his mouth with the precision of an auto mechanic. His nearsighted eyes were fixated on the book. His lips were encircled with ketchup. He held a mangled slice of white bread halfway to his mouth. His receipt book was on the chair next to him.

The music of alienation played a hymn in Mama Celeste's mind as she watched Jeeter eat. She didn't know what to do. The dirtbag said he'd evict her and had to be confronted. There were several ways to go at it. Mama could leave him unmolested until they got outside and then lay into him. That would be the safe thing to do. Keep things private. Keep it discreet. Make sure there were no witnesses, just him and her. Another way was to have it out with him right here in Saint Anthony. Let the shit hit the fan. Putting her arms around the shoebox, Mama Celeste shot to her feet, the chair toppling to the floor. The ruckus caused every head in the room to turn and look.

Jeeter Roche saw her and put the slice of bread on his plate. Prison had taught him quite a few things. The crucial lesson was, don't let anyone slip up on you from behind. The second lesson was even more elementary. There was a totem pole in life. Some folks were high on it. Others were low. But either way, you had to know your place. It was obvious that Mama Celeste wasn't hip to this.

A monk making the rounds mistakenly believed the property manager had nodded off and tapped him on the shoulder. The brown robe stood at the table and said, not unkindly, "I'm sorry, lad, but there's no dozing in the dining room. It's against the house rules. If you need a good kip, take it elsewhere."

"I ain't sleeping, father," Jeeter protested. "I'm resting. I've been working hard lately. I'm pooped out."

"Have you been doing the Lord's work?"

"Each and every day. You wouldn't believe it if I told you, but the truth is, I do his dirty work."

The obese priest lanced Jeeter with an unsparing squint. The cleric's eyes were pellets of straw-colored clay; his shabby robe was rough and woolly. His fingernails were black with dirt. His breath was vile with port wine. "Whatever you do, son, contain your conceit, and always keep the name of Jesus in your thoughts."

"I always do, padre," Jeeter replied as the priest moved on to monitor the patrons at another table. "He's in my receipt book. Him and all the other damn reprobates who owe me money."

Trailing in the priest's wake, Mama Celeste cropped up at Jeeter's table. She put the shoebox on the tabletop and waited until she knew what she wanted to say. Jeeter Roche took advantage of her silence and kissed his lips with his teeth. He put his elbows on the paperback, made a steeple with his fingers and said, "Well, if it isn't Mama Celeste. We've run into each other twice in one day. What a privilege. Care to sit down?"

Mama was too proud to be seated in his presence. "No."

"You want something from me?" he asked.

She stated her claim. "You said you'd evict me."

"Are you referring to us talking this morning?"

"Damn right I am."

Gorged on fiction and powdered eggs, a meal fit for a king, Jeeter undid the top button of his jeans and settled back in his seat. "Don't take things out of context, Mama. I said I'd have to evict you if you didn't pay the rent on time. The law requires me to do that. It's not my choice."

Mama put her hands on the table. "Don't feed me that saccharine. You said you'd throw me out."

"That's untrue. I never said that."

"You know what?"

Jeeter hesitated. "Tell me, I'm all ears."

"You're a goddamn liar."

Jeeter wasn't happy to hear this. His credibility as a drug dealer hinged on his popularity. Someone calling him a liar wasn't good publicity. Someone doing it in Saint Anthony was akin to murder. That was another thing he'd learned in the pen. What other folks thought of you was dire. But he was a landlord. He took people's hard-earned money from them and they hated him. There were only a few things you could count on in life. There was the sun in the morning. There was the moon at night. There was the rent you had to pay until the end of time, and there was Jeeter at your door to collect it. It was a contrary position to be in. He said, "Mama, do you read books?"

Mama Celeste glared at him. Dreadlocks cascaded over her shoulders. "Don't give me that flimflam. I read the newspaper and *Reader's Digest.*"

"Me reading books smartened up my ass. If you don't pay the rent, what am I supposed to do, pay it for you?"

Mama banged her fist on the landlord's plate of food. "I ain't asking you to pay nothing for me. I got money."

Powdered egg bits rocketed off the plate and onto Jeeter's goose down vest. Keeping his temper, he said, "Then what's the damn holdup? May I remind you, that as we speak, you still owe me for this week?"

"I know that."

"Then where's your money? The rent is due."

"You didn't have to threaten me. I have rights, damn it."

The acne scars on Jeeter's cheeks pulsed with blood. He calmed himself by putting his hand on the paperback. He had an insatiable longing to return to the country the author had created. There were gorgeous women in it. Beautiful nights. Lovely flowers were everywhere. It had to be a better place than Saint Anthony Dining Room.

"Rights?" he said. "Wise up, Mama. You don't have any rights. Nobody does. You have choices. That's all you have. And you made the wrong one. I didn't make you not pay the rent. You did what you did out of your own volition. That's democracy."

Democracy was a concept most folks didn't understand. Like the dude Jeeter had sold thirty-seven hits of acid to last month. The guy was a friend of a friend. Seemed like a responsible adult. Paid cash, which was always good. Then Jeeter received word through the grapevine the dunce had transported the hallucinogenic across state lines and had gotten busted in Texas. The LSD had been blue-double-dome, 250 micrograms a tab. Not the finest product on the market. There was talk about it being speedy. But the bottom line was that the fellow didn't have to buy the acid. He didn't have to go to Texas with it. And it was his own fault if he was in prison doing eight years for possession of an illegal substance.

Mama Celeste rebuked him. "There are laws on my side."

"Be real," Jeeter ridiculed. "You know better than that. We're talking about the Allen Hotel. What law? There isn't any. If you want to keep a roof over your head, you'd better play ball with me."

"You're a rotten dog for saying that."

Her condemnation of Jeeter Roche rang out across the dining room with the clarity of a finely delivered trumpet solo. A security guard built along the lines of a heavyweight boxer overheard them and came over to the table to find out what it was about. He got in between Jeeter and Mama and said, "What's going on here?"

Mama stamped her foot. The shoebox jumped an inch off the tabletop. She put her hand on the lid to keep the money from flying out. "Not a damn thing. Him and me are discussing something. Mind your own business."

The guard was taken aback by her miff and puffed out his chest. "This is my business."

"No, it ain't." Mama was losing it and the sensation was delicious. "We're having a private conversation, me and this creep. We don't need you in on it."

"You." The guard waggled a hairy finger at Jeeter. "What's your story?"

Jeeter relished what he was about to say. He arched his eyebrows in feigned innocence, tilted his head, and pouted, "I don't know this broad. Never seen her before in my life. I was just sitting here eating my fucking eggs and reading my damn book and she came up to me and started to bug me. Accused me of all kinds of shit, really hassling me."

"That's a lie," Mama blurted. "Don't make like you don't know me, you bald-headed motherfucker."

"Lady, enough already," the guard said. "We can't have you causing shit. It's against the rules. This is the property of the Catholic Church. You can't do that in here."

The security guard swept Mama Celeste off her feet and dragged her away from the table. Pinning her and the shoebox in a bear hug, he hauled the old woman out of the cafeteria and up the loading ramp to the street, dumping her by the garbage cans on the sidewalk. Saint Anthony maintenance workers were hosing down the pavement, the signal that it was time to push on.

Slowly pulling herself together, Mama moseyed onto lower Jones Street. Every inch of sidewalk was packed with homeless men and women and their dogs and shopping carts. The burned-out hulk of an Oldsmobile without any windows and chrome was at the intersection. The hood was up, the engine gone. Huddled in a doorway was a cluster of Salvadoreño youths talking and drinking wine. Flocks of sea gulls rose and fell over the telephone lines.

As Mama Celeste strolled to Market Street, the wind chased bits of paper. The sun was bivouacked behind two black clouds serrated by the fog. She buttoned the army coat and glanced at the darkening sky. Her mien was distant. She had to find a bathroom quickly.

TWELVE

THE AFTERNOON MOVED ON, galloping toward sundown. The trees, buildings, and automobiles along Market Street were pink, gray, and black. In the smoggy distance was the Maria Alicia Apartments, a three-storied stucco low-income housing project. An SRO hotel used to be at the site—the Gartland Apartments—but it was destroyed in an arson-related fire in December 1975. Twelve residents died in the conflagration. Seventeen others were never found. People said the landlord did it, but nobody could prove it.

Waiting for his wife to emerge from Martuni's Lounge, a Market Street bar, a vexed Jeeter Roche analyzed his marriage. Chiclet had been getting loaded all day long. First the Valium and now Placidyl, a controlled substance classified as a hypnotic. She had downed two pills an hour ago, and when she didn't feel them right away, she took two more. Then it hit her all at once.

How long had him and Chiclet been married, a couple of months? How she carried on, dabbling in dope and messing around with that idiot Stiv Wilkins—as if it was a secret—Jeeter could swear it had been a century. Maybe the age difference between them was the problem. Jeeter had a good twenty-five years on Chiclet, most of them spent in prison.

To complicate things, Chiclet didn't share his love for literature. Books bored her and this pained Jeeter to no end. He couldn't tell his woman about the Brazilian writer Amado. Couldn't tell her about a world that was better than getting high, and better than the one they were living in.

Jeeter saw a police car jet east on Market Street. The cruiser ran the red light on Gough Street, and then the red light on Franklin Street. The sole thing him and her ever talked about was the price of weed. That was his fault. After all he provided the dope and the money and kept her in the drug room to look after their enterprise.

His reverie was cut short as Chiclet, fixing her makeup, paraded out of the bar. The green anorak she had on was skanky and marked with cigarette burns. A quartet of pimples tattooed her chin. Her hair was mussed, draggling over her nose, and getting in the way as she applied cobalt blue lipstick to her mouth.

Richard Rood studied the dope dealer and his wife from behind a parked Saturn sedan. They were a diorama of white people and their problems. He could see them in a museum of the future: urban primitives and their mating rites. They were fools is what they were. He gobbled at them, his gravelly voice carrying across the street: "Yo, baby, yo."

Jeeter froze when he heard Rood. Nothing was worse than that man. Not pestilence. Not disease. Not starvation. Not even death. Too bad the black dealer wasn't a figment of his imagination, the aftermath of taking too many drugs and seeing too many things that weren't there. "Goddamn it," he said to Chiclet, pinching her arm. "We've got company."

Eating up the asphalt in his Timberland boots, Richard Rood made a beeline toward the Allen's property manager. His eyes were somber. His fists were balled. Four inches shorter and fifty pounds lighter than the white man, he transmitted enough hatred to scare the heebie-jeebies out of Jeeter Roche.

Richard gazed at Jeeter, targeting him with a reptilian stare that had taken thousands of hours to perfect in front of a mirror. "I've been looking for you, boy. Been wanting to talk to your ass."

Jeeter was in a lightweight North Face goose down parka held together with duct tape. Corralling his emotions into a semblance of coolness, he twisted his chapped lips and answered, "I could care fucking less. You know why?"

"Why?"

"You were at my house earlier and you were messing with Chiclet, you turd, that's why. What the fuck is wrong with you? You lost your mind or what?"

Richard was terse. "You got something to say about it?"

Jeeter could smell the shabbiness of Richard's patent leather suit. "Yeah, I do. This is my wife we're talking about. What did you have to freak her out for? It was unnecessary. You're out of line."

Richard was nonchalant and hawked a lunger on the ground. "I didn't do nothing untowardly to her."

"Bullshit." Jeeter was excited. "You were trying to intimidate her."

"Who says? That cow?" Richard Rood picked his nose and then motioned at Chiclet. "She's all high."

Jeeter's goose down parka billowed in the wind. "You seriously suck, dude. You've got no respect for nobody or nothing. You're an animal."

"Too bad." Richard spread his arms, indicating serenity. "You dig me?" Nourished by the mounting acrimony, he offered an invitation. It seemed like the manly thing to do. Move the debate to a higher level. A tremor of undiluted hate blanched his face when he said, "You want to fight?"

Jeeter flung the parka on the sidewalk like a bullfighter's cape. "Hell, yeah. I can't have you dogging my old lady."

Taking the initiative was Jeeter's first mistake. The combatants squared off under the streetlights and Richard made contact. He lashed out at Jeeter, feinting left hooks, and connecting with right jabs in the gut, all the while saying, "C'mon, you want a piece of me? What are you waiting for?"

Jeeter retreated a pace, windmilling his arms. Getting jabbed in the stomach hurt. Made him want to toss his cookies. He wasn't ready for no boxing match—and that became his second mistake. Richard snapped off a punch that clipped Jeeter on the nose; a gout of blood streamed from the white dealer's nostrils as he rocked back on his heels.

Richard Rood crowed, "You gonna cry, little pussy? You want your mommy?"

Afraid that Jeeter would get pulverized, Chiclet stepped in between Richard and her husband. Her neck was buried to the chin in a cashmere scarf. The anorak's upturned collar scalloped her high-boned cheeks. The wind coming off the street had burned her skin crimson red. She placed a hand on her hip and said to Richard Rood, "What do you want from me and Jeeter?"

Richard dropped his fists and targeted her with a disingenuous smile. A smile that had several subtexts: repugnance, interest, and abhorrence. He schooled his eyes on Chiclet's body with undisguised and scientific interest. He'd never been with a woman. Not in the Biblical sense. Technically, he was a virgin. Wouldn't know a vagina if it hit him in the face. Personally speaking, he was a child of sodomy.

He examined her breasts, their roundness showing through a ratty cardigan ski sweater. He appraised the lines of her buttocks bunched inside a pair of melon pink capris. He measured the narrowness of her ankles and the Indian sandals on her feet, the emerald green nail polish on her toenails. She was as queer to him as an alien from another galaxy.

Chiclet brushed away a strand of dyed blonde hair from her triangular face. Richard's belladonna black eyes made her head reel. He was more unnerving than a bad acid trip. It was like flirting with a rattlesnake. If you ventured too close, you'd get bitten and die. She blustered, "So what do you want?"

"What do I want?" Richard read her body language and said with impatience, "You need to do something about them pimples, you hear me? But fuck it. Let's get down to brass tacks. I'm looking for someone."

Chiclet had broken the thread of violence. Plasma trickled out of Jeeter's busted nose, proof that his hardness was complete fabrication. He was too old for brawling. Jeeter pointed one foot at Richard. His left shoulder was hitched high. His slanted feline eyes were askew.

There wasn't anything about him that was in sync. He said, "Who's that? Anybody we know?"

Richard was emphatic. "Damn it, yeah. It's a buddy of yours. One of your honchos."

"And who would that be, huh? Who do you know that we know? You and me ain't got shit in common."

"Yes, we do. This white dude."

"Most of my friends are white. Which one are you talking about?"

"That punk rock faggot."

Jeeter's resistance was melting faster than ice cream left out on the hot pavement. Tiredness tickled his throat. It was nightmarish to have Richard Rood breathing down your neck. Wanting to put an end to it, Jeeter ventured, "You mean Stiv Wilkins?"

Richard's eyes softened. "Uh huh. I mean Stiv."

"He ain't my buddy."

"He ain't? What exactly is he to you?"

"The pissant is just a tenant in my building."

"Your building? You own it?"

"No."

"Then what does that make you?"

"I oversee the Allen and all the shit that goes down in it."

"Is that so? You must be one very important motherfucker in the scene over there."

"I am."

"But you do know Stiv, don't you?"

Jeeter confessed without shame. "I admit to that."

"Well, then." Richard Rood stroked his chin sagaciously. He toed a beer can into the gutter. "I'm looking for the dickhead. Have you seen him?"

"Damn, right, I have." Jeeter said. His tongue burned with a snitch's lust to be truth speaking. He practically strangled on the words when they petered out of his mouth. "The fucking runt sold me a lousy gun earlier. He said it was good. I believed him. Then I went to test it at the Lake Merced shooting range and the thing exploded in my hand."

"No shit?"

"Stiv's a goddamn lizard. He sucks. I hate him."

"But where is he?"

Jeeter Roche unbuttoned his shirt and used the tails to soak up the blood on his face. "How the hell would I know?"

There was little else to say. Richard wanted to insult Jeeter, just to fuck with him, but decided to reserve his energy. Cooler that he should hold back and stay blasé. He said, "Okay."

The flu had him going downstream in a river of incomprehension. His fists were sore from rearranging Jeeter's face. He didn't know what his next step was, but it wasn't hanging around these dolts. He had no time for trashy-assed losers. Jeeter and his woman were good for doodly squat. Richard Rood bid them a curt farewell. "Hey, I didn't mean to fuck with your evening or bring you down, but it had to be done, you know?"

THIRTEEN

O NCE YOU GOT OUT of the Tenderloin and into the Castro district, Market Street became a different palette of colors. Few homeless people were seen. No crack dealers hawked their wares. No fire engines raced to tenement hotels. No hookers were at the curb. In their stead were renovated Victorians, upscale flower shops, jewelry stores, pricey restaurants, hair salons, and wine bars.

The annual Castro Street festival was taking place during the upcoming weekend, and a hundred thousand people would congregate outside to party. The disco king Sylvester used to sing at the event and had regaled the masses with his opus "You Make Me Feel (Mighty Real)."

The song was an anthem for gay men in San Francisco and was played a hundred times a day in neighborhood bars. Sylvester was the reigning diva of the international dance music scene in the 1980s. Recording for a regional label, his pioneering vocals made their presence felt in nightclubs from New York to Berlin. He died of AIDS, as did thousands in the city.

At four o'clock the doors to the post office were open, in the hopes of attracting a breeze. Sunlight had penetrated the station's blue-tinted plate-glass walls; ponds of light coruscated on the brick tile floor. An airmail package with foreign stickers sat next to a computerized cash register on the service counter. A muzak version of the Lee Morgan composition "Sidewinder" percolated from a radio.

The lone clerk at the counter, a middle-aged Filipino man, heard a person come in the door. He levered his head to see who it was. The afternoon had been slow and he was a mite bored. It was a male customer, one he hadn't seen before. Postal work was like that—people came and went, never to be seen again. There were too many faces to remember, too many voices to sort out. Some brought good cheer along with their mail. Most didn't.

As the man's footsteps came closer, the clerk's short black hair stood up on end. His lips curled, showing uneven teeth. His skin whitened from brown to gray. His eyes widened in tortured recognition when he saw what was in the fellow's hand.

A clean-shaven Stiv Wilkins pointed a Colt revolver with a three-inch barrel at the postal worker's pudgy face. With his hair combed, Stiv looked positively juvenile, no more than eighteen. He pulled back the gun's hammer, cleared his throat of phlegm and stated the purpose of his visit. "Can you help me, please?"

"To do-do-do-do what?" the clerk stuttered.

"Open the register drawer."

"Why?"

Stiv was direct. "I want the money."

"I can't give it to you."

Stiv was perplexed and signified with the Colt. "Why not?"

"Because you have to make a purchase. You have to put in money. It won't open otherwise."

"Fuck that." Stiv goaded him in the chin with the revolver.

The clerk had coronary thrombosis written over his face. His orbs were egg yolks swimming in blood vessels. His skin was greasier than bacon. The sweat stains in his blue postal uniform were moons. He made a suggestion. "How about buying some stamps?"

Stiv let his arm drop, the gun at his side. His tongue was metallic, a warning that an attack was coming on. Not a full-blown hallucination, but near enough. The walls shifted a few inches. The post office's bulletin board, spangled with the FBI's Most Wanted posters, was moving up and down. It let him know he was on the brink.

Closing his eyes, Stiv forgot where he was. He daydreamed about taking the cable car at Powell and Market over Nob Hill and down into Chinatown. The ride took forever and you could see Angel Island and Mount Tamalpais. He reopened his eyes and found the postal worker was on all fours under the stamp machine. A handful of coins, dimes, pennies, and nickels were on the floor next to a stack of boxes. Stiv asked sleepily, not quite sure what was going on, "Where's the money?"

"I'm trying," the man gasped, "to get change for stamps."

Having no more patience for the situation, Stiv scrambled on the countertop by the weight scale and sighted the clerk with the Colt. He counted backwards from ten and when he reached zero, he asked himself a question. Where had the summer gone? June had been cold and foggy. July had been a month without heat at the Allen Hotel. In August you had to hide out from the tourists on Market Street. Now it was a melancholy September day in his heart. Stiv fired the gun, once, twice, three, four times.

When a man is shot in the neck, his head explodes in a dance of bone fragments. Pieces of his skull take flight. How far the body parts fly depends on how close the shooter is to the victim. The brain splatters like jelly. The eyes pop out. The face is ruined in a surge of skin and blood. The lower cavities vacate urine and feces. By the time the gunshot's amplitude dies away, the body is already turning cold.

The postal guy was kissing the ground, praying in Spanish. "*Madre de Dios, por favor . . .*"

All Stiv heard was a click—the pistol's safety button was on. He undid the safety, and came up with a better idea. If he couldn't send the postman to glory, at least he could kill himself. He flipped the pistol around and put the muzzle in his mouth. Wedding his lips to the barrel, Stiv rimmed the bore with his tongue, and hit the trigger.

Shooting yourself in the face is the pièce de résistance of suicide. It's a hostile act that guarantees a drastic mess for someone to clean up. Believing he was dead, Stiv was puzzled. In the afterlife there was supposed to be no jazz on the radio, but nonetheless he was hearing it in the background. And the clerk was futzing with the stamp machine. Nothing had changed, meaning he was alive. Stiv had a gander at the Colt: it had been unloaded.

Hopping off the counter, he backpedaled out of the post office and cut up Eighteenth Street, just as the sun dipped over the sparsely grassed fields of the Eureka Valley Playground. He bustled past Cliff's Variety hardware store and the Castro Theater and made a break for Market Street. Tongue lolling from his mouth, Stiv Wilkins spurted across the road and passed under an elm tree, trying to outrun the hallucination that was overtaking him.

Fog was coming down over the forested hills onto the beach as the skiff neared the cove. Harbor seals swam alongside the boat, their sleek heads visible in the moonlight. Mallard ducks were quacking in the water. José Reyna watched the two Ohlone oarsmen as they paddled the craft. Their unbraided black hair was wet with sweat and they were barefoot in wool trousers. Their thick leather belts held butcher knives and muzzle-loading pistols. The buoyant skiff, woven from marsh reeds, nosed into a wave. Two-Fingered Tom cleaned his guns and said to José, "*Chale*, this is a bitch, ain't it?"

The last time Two-Fingered Tom had been in San Francisco, he'd escaped from jail. Since there was a bounty for his capture, he didn't look forward to returning to the village and stared at the piney hillsides with suspicion. The two outlaws sat in the boat's prow, attempting to keep their weapons and gunpowder dry. The rest of José's men, *mestizos* and runaway Mission Indian slaves, were in Oakland guarding their horses.

The first Ohlone oarsman was using his paddle as a tiller, urging the vessel toward the coastline. Three yards from the shore, the other Ohlone jumped into the surf and guided the boat onto the sand. José and Two-Fingered Tom grabbed their serapes, rifles, and quirts and put on their sombreros.

"What's the name of this beach?" José asked.

"Warm Water Cove," Two-Fingered said.

The skiff was hidden onshore behind a crop of scrub brush and camouflaged with tree branches. José watched the Indians as they searched the ground for the path that led through the pine forest and into San Francisco. The older Ohlone was muscular; his back was cicatrized with scars from the whippings he'd received at Mission Dolores. The younger Indian, slim and quick on his feet, said something to him in pidgin Spanish and then gave the high sign. He said, "*Aquí, hombres.*"

Two-Fingered muttered, "That *pinche indio* better know where he's taking us."

With the moon in the west to navigate by, the four men followed the trail into the trees. The Ohlone took the lead. Two-Fingered Tom, paranoid out of his mind, brought up the rear with a six-barreled squirrel rifle. It was a model favored by the gringos. Birds were tweeting in a lilac bush. Two deer, a doe and a fawn, ran away when they heard the men. A small bear crashed through chokeberry bush brambles and a coyote barked in the hills.

An hour went by before the outlaws broke out of the forest and into a clearing. The ground had been fenced off for pasture; Spanish cattle raised their horned heads at the interlopers. Two-Fingered signed with his hands at the Ohlone. The Indian with the scars on his back pointed to a creek that ran north. Two-Fingered said to José, "We follow the *agua* and then in a couple of miles we get to the Mission."

Resuming their march, the bandits proceeded to walk alongside the creek. They encountered more cows, a herd of sheep, and a gang of wild dogs. Two-Fingered Tom was taking swigs from a flask of absinthe and singing a *corrido*. He couldn't wait to find the Chinamen in the village—they sold the best opium he'd ever smoked.

The march was uneventful until they saw the white walls and church tower of Mission Dolores. The settlement dated back to the 1770s and was one of the oldest in the state of California. It was ringed with corrals and outbuildings that housed the overseers and other church employees. Further off were the shanties of the Mission Indians. Small plots of corn, squash, and beans bordered the creek. Horses were grazing on burdock. A half-breed boy, naked from the waist down, spied the strangers and ran past the corrals into the cornfields.

The young Ohlone held up his hand and made the travelers get behind a ridge of serpentine—several lawmen on horseback were riding out of the compound. The horses kicked up dirt and José Reyna was hard pressed to keep from sneezing. When the horsemen had ridden down the road and into the woods, the guides led him and Two-Fingered Tom to a side gate. In front of them was a cemetery. Rose bushes climbed the adobe walls; stone grave markers were corroding in the loamy soil. The two Ohlone stopped and talked to each other in their native tongue. The older man drew a circle in the dirt with his finger and then crossed it out.

Two-Fingered Tom said to José, "He's saying there are too many ghosts around here. Ohlone slaves are buried in that graveyard. Their spirits want out of the ground."

Retreating into a corral, the *pistoleros* hid behind a bale of hay and prepared their weapons. José had an 1836 Colt Navy repeating revolver. The Ohlone carried old-fashioned flintlock pistols. Two-Fingered Tom's adolescent face was stern under his sombrero as he said, "*Orale*, this has been long overdue."

The mission's stout wood gate opened and a man in cowboy clothes with a Sharps rifle stepped out. He was bearded and wore a cream-colored ten-gallon Stetson hat. He looked at the cemetery and at the cows by the creek. He stared at the cornfields and at the corral where the outlaws were hidden. José was sure they'd been seen. But the guard didn't detect them and shouldered his rifle and went back inside the walls. A few minutes later a priest came out.

"That's him," Two-Fingered Tom exclaimed.

The brown-robe started walking down the dirt road toward the Mission lagoon. He was fat and bald with a face that was red from drink; his nose was bulbous and his mouth was thin. His leather sandals raised sprites of dust. The hem of his garment was muddy. In his right hand he clutched a staff carved from hemlock wood. Around his waist was a rope belt. From it hung a deerskin pouch.

Two-Fingered Tom said, "This is it, *vatos*. Watch my back."

The outlaw, skinnier than a scarecrow, two-stepped out from behind the hay. He brushed off his leather chaps and jacket and greeted the cleric as if they were old friends. "*Oye, padre, ¿qué pasa?*" Extracting the flask from his jacket, Two-Fingered had a lusty pull from it and offered it to the priest. "You want some, *viejo*? The shit's good for you, eh? Puts hair on your *cojones*."

The brown-robe said, "Who are you, *hijo*?"

"I ain't a friend, that's all you got to know."

A pinto pony nickered in the corral. A cow mooed in the fields. A rooster began to cock-a-doodle-doo. Two-Fingered Tom put the flask in his belt and tapped the priest on the chest with his squirrel gun. "Gimme the *chingadera*, that pouch you got, *tu pinche gusano*."

The two Indians jumped up and pinioned the brown-robe. The younger Ohlone removed the pouch and handed it to Two-Fingered Tom. The teenaged desperado untied it and poured the contents into his palm. It was three ounces of gold dust from the mines near Mokelumne Hill.

The scarred Indian withdrew a knife from his belt and ran it over the priest's face, testing the blade's sharpness against the man's white skin. José Reyna went to stop him, but his cousin held him back, saying, "No, *vato*. Let him do what he's got to do."

The Ohlone drove the blade in the brown-robe's chest; the man's legs kicked once, a hiss of breath escaped from his mouth, and that was it. The mockingbirds in the cedar grove next to the cemetery began to protest. Two-Fingered Tom sifted the gold dust back into the pouch and tucked it in his shirt. Disregarding the dead priest, he said to José, "Let's go, *hombre*. We've got a lot of shit to accomplish."

FOURTEEN

THE SIX O'CLOCK TELEVISION NEWS reported that a cache of the Brinks cash, about a hundred thousand dollars, had been recovered from under a car on Polk Street. The money, wrapped in butcher paper, had been run over several times during the day and no longer resembled hard currency. A spokeswoman for the Brinks firm claimed the sum was a miniscule percentage of what had been stolen.

The sun had taken a nosedive over the Golden Gate Bridge into the ocean. A foghorn pealed in the bay near the Marin Headlands. Fog swooped over Corona Heights. A westerly wind bent the trees on Market Street; garbage did a fandango on the sidewalk.

A hooker was working the parking lot behind the French bistro at Franklin and Market. She was youngish, about thirty-five. The rouge on her face was cracking, chipping off in flakes. Her hair, bleached bone white, frothed over a high forehead. Her emerald green eyes were slits in violet-hued mascara. She had on a red leather mini-skirt and a waist-length rabbit fur jacket. Under the skirt were two miles of bare legs. Under the jacket there was nothing at all.

The intersection at Franklin was a good spot for a girl to work. The street was one-way. The stoplight was lengthy, giving motorists and prostitutes an ample opportunity to check each other out. But the only people who consistently made use of the corner were homeless panhandlers, mostly black and white women over forty.

Mama Celeste saw the hooker and decided to introduce herself. Waddling over to the parking lot, she was wheezing and her feet were sore. Orthopedic shoes were a mistake. They didn't do a thing to help you. She loosened the muffler from her neck, flicked a dreadlock off her face. Shivering in the army jacket, she was dressed no better than a wino. Her kinky hair was flattened under a handkerchief and a Giants baseball hat. Her ankle-high shoes had rents in them. Her stockings were past their peak. Her dress had been around since the days of the Roman Empire. Her teeth were gritty from the dirt in the street. Was she *meshugge* to give away the money in the shoebox? Her parents would roll over in their graves if they saw what she was doing.

The whore didn't acknowledge the old woman. Instead she concentrated on the cars. Headlights were brilliant in the fogged out blackness and haloed her. A Jeep Cherokee skated to the curb and the driver, a twenty-something white guy in a leather bomber jacket, rolled down the window. She had a few words with him, nodded a no, and he drove off.

A spear point of loneliness tweaked Mama. Where was her husband now? Was he in heaven? Did they allow black people in there nowadays? Chances were, they did, and she'd find him waiting for her with open arms. Mama saw that she wasn't going to get anywhere with the working girl, so when the light at the corner turned green, she gallivanted across Market Street.

A pigeon with no legs was pecking at the grass in the pavement. The bird's feathers had clotted into clumps. Its tiny head was beleaguered with tumors. Its beak had hairline fractures in it. It schlepped along the pavement by using its wings as if they were feet. It nibbled at the scraggly grass, not liking the taste of it.

Seeing Mama Celeste walk by, the pigeon went inert. It didn't have the energy to fly off. It was tired how Tenderloin pigeons got tired, having to dodge traffic all day long. Eating trash to stay alive. Getting sprayed with pesticides by the city's sanitation workers. Fighting other birds for turf. Keeping homeless people and tourists and cops from stepping on you. The struggle was never ending and exhausting. The pigeon couldn't wait to find a nook or cranny to sleep in, even if it was just for a few minutes.

Mama Celeste spotted the troubled creature and regarded it with pity. The bird was a double amputee and had eyes that were almost human. She said to it, "What's with you, all by yourself out here. You must be lonely, ha?"

The pigeon quailed when she spoke. It looked up at the old lady with a crazed, abject expression. It expected abuse and was ready for the worst. It was a ghetto bird, underprivileged and with low self-esteem.

Prying the lid off the shoebox, Mama extracted a twenty-dollar bill. Bowing from the waist, she invited the bird to take it. "For you," she said respectfully. "It's all I have. The money might do you good."

The pigeon gave Mama Celeste a depressive, hard-boiled glance, and then browsed over the cash. It was totally confused. Money meant nothing to a pigeon. But a gift was a gift. You couldn't refuse it. That would be rude. And maybe dumb. You never knew. Upright on its leg stumps, the pigeon took the twenty from Mama's fingers. It trilled once, spread its balding wings, and flew away with the Andrew Jackson in its beak.

Mama Celeste watched the legless pigeon sweep over the rooftops and then resumed her pilgrimage up Market Street. The white neon cross on the First Baptist Church was a beacon in the fog. An overturned turquoise-blue Ford Fiesta with no doors was ablaze next to Martuni's Lounge. Green and gold dragonflies rode the currents around the burning car; the stench of deliquescent plastic was a tight fitting glove on the street.

Night had fallen on forty thousand homeless people, the vacant office buildings on Market Street, the clock tower at the Embarcadero, and the icy black-green waters in the San Francisco Bay.

Richard Rood trailed Mama Celeste, keeping his distance. A lone one-hundred-dollar bill was suspended from the woman's coat sleeve.

A Ulysses S. Grant was stuck on her collar. She was leaving a line of twenty-dollar bills on the ground behind her. Richard was scooping them up as he walked. "The sister is a fucking whack-o," he said to himself. "She's out of her damn tree."

A hag such as Mama Celeste was an automatic victim in his book. In the food chain of crime, she was a target. She was ripe for the plucking. But she had given him money with no strings attached. Nobody had ever done anything like that for Richard and he had to return the favor. His code of honor demanded payback. It was a complicated twist of fate. He couldn't rob her. He couldn't steal her cash. He had to protect her.

The third man Richard Rood killed had been at the Expansion Bar, a working-class tavern off Church Street. An NBA playoff basketball game was on the television and the patrons were watching it. Richard had gotten himself a stool and was in the act of sitting down. Someone tap-tapped him on the shoulder, hard enough to put him on the alert. He turned around to find a drunken white guy with a beard. The dude was apoplectic; his skin was tomato red. He said to Richard, "That's my old lady's chair, you dick. You took it from her."

Richard was congenial, seeing that the white man was angry. He removed his hindquarters from the stool and said, "No problem, cool breeze. She can take it. Have a nice day."

The drunk clutched the seat and walked away, saying, "Fucking queer."

Pulling out a knife, a cheesy Mexican-made sticker, Richard jammed it in the guy's neck until only the handle was visible. He must have nicked an artery because a fountain of blood bloomed on his victim's shirt. The fellow fell to the floor and his girlfriend caterwauled. The bartender got on the phone to call the police. Richard said adios without causing any further commotion.

The old black lady with the money needed a guardian angel. Out here in the street with these lunatics running around—people would kill you for a cigarette—there was no telling what might happen to her. Pushing through the fog to the Allen Hotel, Richard

Rood swore an oath. Not only was he going to kick Stiv Wilkins's ass into kingdom come, he'd murder anyone that tried to run off with the biddy's shoebox. He smiled from the bottom of his soul. The vow, complete with the threat of mayhem, made him happier than he'd been all day.

Mama Celeste and then Richard Rood passed the ghost of the poet Jack Micheline on Market Street. Hunching over a tailor-made cigarette, Micheline's white hair riffled in the wind. His cargo jacket was zipped to the neck. His khaki trousers were slung low on his hips. His shoes were dusty. His smooth-shaven skin was slick with beads of perspiration. He extracted a kitchen match from his jacket, ignited the match's tip with his thumbnail, and drew the flame over the fag's tip. His profile threw an enormous silhouette on the wall behind him. The shine in his brown eyes came not from him, but from a lone streetlight. He sucked furiously on the fag, taking quick tokes while planning how to get to his room at the Civic Center Hotel on Twelfth Street.

Though his friend Jack Kerouac achieved greater fame, there was a period during the 1950s when Jack Micheline was better known in underground literary circles. In later years, unwilling to capitalize on the hype of the Beat Generation, he stayed in a series of SRO hotels before dying in 1998.

Restaurant seekers clogged the pavement and made it impossible for Jack Micheline to walk. Throngs of well-dressed middle-class young women and men blocked his path. Nobody noticed him—ghosts were difficult to see in the dark. He mooched against a chain-link fence and smoked and watched the street. He observed the drunks sleepwalking out of the Zuni Café. He saw the television transmission tower in the mists on Twin Peaks. A fragment of a poem tiptoed through his leonine head and he chased after it. He wasn't in any hurry to find it. The night was long and he had all the time in the universe.

The Brinks dough had been missing for thirteen hours.

FIFTEEN

A N EXHAUSTED STIV WILKINS found a bench under a dwarf palm tree in Dolores Park and sprawled on it. The park sat on a hill and commanded an excellent view of the city. The only things Stiv recognized in the skyline were the General Hospital and the jail at the Hall of Justice on 850 Bryant Street. The mean-spirited felony tank windows were discernible from miles away.

On the other side of the park were the copper-faceted dome of the Second Church of Christ, Scientist, and a row of apartment houses. One of the buildings had been the home of Emma Goldman, the Russian-born anarchist orator and writer. In the summer of 1916 she was taken to jail after the arrests of Warren Billings and Tom Mooney. Later she was deported to Russia in the aftermath of the Palmer Raids of 1919.

Stiv's half a year in the city prison had been enough. Eating baloney sandwiches three times a day—the dogs on death row at the SPCA had a better diet. Wiping your privates with last week's newspapers on a broken toilet. Sleeping with one eye open to make sure a cellmate didn't steal your shoes. Taking a shower once a week with ten other guys. Stiv had outgrown the routine.

Unearthing an overripe orange from his pants, a memento from a restaurant dumpster, Stiv peeled the fruit with his switchblade and ate it. He rearranged the Colt revolver in his belt and put the knife back in his boot. Then he doffed his motorcycle jacket, rolled it into a pillow, and stretched out on the bench.

He'd fucked up at the post office, which had been predictable. Robbery had never been his forte. Neither was using or selling guns. But the real issue was this: What was he good at? He was twenty-five years old with no job or nothing. So what was wrong with him? Maybe he just wasn't meant for great things. It was hard to accept that. He had dreams, little ones.

The highlight of Stiv's career had been his band's last show at a club on Geary Street. The venue was a deconsecrated synagogue with stained glass windows and a hardwood dance floor that could hold a thousand people. Before that it was the former headquarters of the People's Temple, the church founded by Jim Jones, the charismatic preacher who'd led his flock into mass suicide in Guyana.

Stiv had been drunk on vodka because he was self-conscious, and speeding on crystal for the energy. He was shirtless and had slashed himself in the chest with a broken Budweiser beer bottle. The microphone was in his mouth; the cord was tied around his neck. He was screeching at the top of his lungs, trying to hear himself over the guitars, the feedback, the drummer who wasn't keeping time, and the bass that threatened to blow out the monitors.

The lead guitarist went into a repetitive one-note solo that ended when he broke a string and smashed his Gibson against an amplifier—the guitar's neck splintered and Stiv caught a sliver in the thigh. All the kids roared at the sight of his blood. Holding the mike stand over his head, he flung it into the crowd. Other kids were climbing onto the stage; a fan had his arms around Stiv's boots and was kissing them.

Maybe he had something to offer the world. If a moth could turn into a butterfly, he could too. And, he mimicked himself, if he lived long enough, Norbert Deflass would put him back on Haldol. San Francisco had thousands of crazy people in the streets. California had closed a large percentage of its mental institutions in the 1970s and the city had become an open-air insane asylum. But that wasn't going to be Stiv's fate. "No way," he vowed.

It was a false promise. With a hallucination's unrelenting logic, Stiv Wilkins was slowly divided in two. His body was moored to the bench, but his spirit zipped out of his head in a slew of unfamiliar voices and he fainted.

Beating a retreat from the brown-robe's corpse, José Reyna and Two-Fingered Tom and the two Ohlone walked into a stand of Ponderosa pine. Skirting the Dolores lagoon, a marshy body of water that several creeks bled into, they evaded a quartet of Indian slaves fishing on the shore.

Two-Fingered kept his crippled hand on the squirrel gun's trigger. Blue jays, robins, starlings, and sparrows dithered in the trees. It was getting on his nerves. His soft-soled riding boots were making footprints in the mud. If the *pinche* gringos wanted to find them, it wouldn't be too hard. A blind man could see their tracks.

On the south side of the lagoon were a general store, a blacksmith's shop, a saloon with a hotel, and a barbershop. The sad-faced wood shingled buildings abutted a two-way dirt road. The Ohlone guides motioned José and Two-Fingered toward a rise behind the saloon, a low hill that was dotted with weeping willows. The outlaws secured cover behind the willows and looked at the bay. The masts of British frigates and U.S. warships blackwashed the piers at the Embarcadero. To the north were the chimneys on Telegraph Hill.

"I need to get hold of some goddamn opium," Two-Fingered said.

Below them was a courthouse with a rude log cabin jail. Three Miwok Indian women were sitting on the courthouse steps begging for food. A mangy dog was gnawing on a steer bone at their feet. Two-Fingered Tom slapped José on the leg and said in an undertone, "*Mira*, over yonder."

A dozen gringos in low-heeled cowboy boots, flannel shirts, and denim jeans were assembled under a gigantic oak tree with a priest. In front of them was a Mexican with his hands tied behind his back. His white linen shirt was torn; his pants were undone. His left eye was swollen. Blood dripped from his shoulder-length black hair onto his bronzed shoulders. The cleric was holding a crucifix.

One of the cowboys, a man with a blonde mustache and piercing blue eyes, threw a rope over the oak's upper branches. He gave the rope a tug and constructed a hangman's noose from it. Another cowboy took a Sharps rifle and smacked the Mexican in the head with the weapon's butt; two other cowboys placed the noose around his neck.

The local magistrate, a tall, potbellied white man in a gray pinstriped suit, mud-splattered spats, and a beaver skin top hat, addressed the Mexican. "You are Antonio Valencia?"

"Yeah, that's me."

"You want to live?"

"What do you think, *pendejo*?"

"Then you'd better tell us where José Reyna is."

The Mexican said nothing and the cowboys heaved the rope. The prisoner was lifted three feet off the ground; his face turned a violent shade of green. The magistrate made a signal with his thumb; the cowboys holding the rope let it go slack and the Mexican fell in the dirt. He coughed up blood and rolled over on his back, foaming at the mouth. The priest waved the crucifix over him and said a few words in Latin.

Two-Fingered Tom tapped the squirrel gun's walnut stock. "*Pinche maricones.* Where the fuck do they get off with this foolishness?" He said to José, "Do you know the *vato* they're lynching? They're making like the motherfucker rides with us."

José Reyna saw the seeds of death in Two-Fingered's coal black eyes, and knew he had the same look in his own eyes. When you were close to *muerte*, ghosts came out of no place. José's dead wife haunted him and brought sorrow. He replied, "I've never seen the *ese* before."

A cowboy got the Mexican to his feet, and the noose was placed around the prisoner's neck again. His *mestizo* face, more Indian than Spanish, was becalmed, as if he'd made peace with his demise. He turned to the sun and saw a heron fly over the lagoon. Crickets chirped in the tule reeds. The man in the top hat snapped his fingers, prompting the cowboys—and the Mexican went up in the air. He gyrated, fighting the noose, using his chin to keep it from strangling him. His feet went up and down, as if he were pedaling a bicycle.

"That's enough," the magistrate said.

The Mexican slammed into the ground. The judge stood over him and bellowed, "This is your last chance. Where's that goddamn horse thief?"

The dearth of oxygen in the condemned man's brain had muted his tongue. Too groggy to talk, he struggled with his bonds. The white men were staring at him while the brown-robe gave him last rites. The rope was positioned around the prisoner's abraded neck for the third time. The birds in the tree's branches made a frightful racket. The judge cried, "Heave ho!" and the Mexican was strung up. He did a mazurka in mid-air, his feet seeking the earth.

Two-Fingered Tom let loose with all six barrels of the squirrel gun. Designed to hunt small game, the carbine was accurate. The fusillade cleaved through the judge's hat and wounded three cowboys. The gringos returned the fire, pulverizing the weeping willows. With bullets flying everywhere, the Ohlone led Two-Fingered and José Reyna into a thicket. California's most wanted criminals retraced their steps back to Warm Water Cove. They got in the skiff and crossed the bay to the friendlier shores of Oakland.

A hysterical car horn on Dolores Street jolted Stiv out of his swoon. He opened his eyes and saw the horizon had deepened from aqua blue into indigo. The bald hills of Berkeley and Oakland were lampblack. The skies over the oil refineries in Richmond were marigold yellow. The Bay Bridge was gridlocked with rush hour commuters. An unmarked twin-prop military intelligence plane and a full moon were poised over Market Street. Sitting up, he put on his motorcycle jacket.

He wanted nothing more than to sit on the bench and savor the evening's breeze, to let it be a barrier between him and what was coming, but the clock was ticking away. The rent had to be paid. Securing the gun in his belt, Stiv levitated to his feet and made his way down a slope to the park's water fountain for a drink.

SIXTEEN

RICHARD ROOD DUCKED INTO Martuni's Lounge to use the rest-room. As he came in the door, dodging the neon sign that spelled out the watering hole's name, he scanned the joint. You never knew when you might run into someone you didn't want to see. Cops. Probation officers. Ex-lovers. The dudes you burned on drug deals. Several patrons, two women and a man, were at the bar. A jazz pianist was playing standards at one end of the room. A television was tuned to the news.

The guards at a Wells Fargo Bank branch on Mission Street had detained a sixty-year old Salvadoreño man about the Brinks money. He was in possession of seventy thousand dollars. The cash was in his coat. He said he didn't know where it came from. Then he recanted his testimony and said he found it on a sidewalk in the Tenderloin. The police had issued a statement: No comment. There would be an update at ten o'clock.

While urinating in the latrine, Richard probed his face in the mirror. The flu was getting to him. Doing him cosmetic damage. He had ashy skin. Fried eyes and hair all dry. The lines on his forehead were getting deeper. Double chin was bigger. Mouth like a glory hole. Nothing nice. He shook a few drops of piss from his dick, buttoned up his pants, and walked out of the bar.

Back on Market Street he ran into a good-looking white man under a streetlamp. The gent was in a costly two-tone gray-green suit, glossy brogans and a red beret; his hair was cut in bangs across his forehead. His complexion was marble white. He seemed to be trying to hook up with some rough trade. He was putting out the signs: hanging in the shadows, keeping quiet, acting wistful.

Knowing he could earn a few bucks turning a trick if he played his cards right, Richard glissaded over to the white dude. He was all smiles and sugary pressure. He laid it on thick, waxing seductive. "Hey, girlfriend, you want some company? I'll make it worth your while."

The man gave Richard a taste of his scrumptious profile and didn't say anything. Richard knew he was being tested. It didn't faze him. On the contrary, it turned him on. "What's your name?" he asked.

Richard Rood had made it with all kinds of men. He'd been with Puerto Ricans from New York City and with Creole boys from New Orleans, cowboys from Wyoming and hobos from Florida. He'd been with white studs and black dudes. He'd done it in restrooms, park bushes, under train trestles, in hotel rooms. But he'd never gotten down with a rich white man.

He gambled and gave the stranger a kiss. The fellow's lips were cold and unresponsive. Encircling the man's waspish waist with his hands, he pressed himself against his cock. It was limp. Richard kissed him again, this time more violently, putting his teeth and tongue into it. He asked, "You okay? You feeling it?" He added, "Let's get real here. You got a hankering to go to bed with me? It'll cost you. I'm good and I'm expensive."

A light bulb went on in Richard's brain. Maybe the guy wanted to have sex right there in the street. Maybe he needed titillation. Needed to do it up against a parking meter. Wanted it rough. Disengaging his arms, Richard took the man's hand and said, "Look, it's fifty for head, a hundred to go all the way. You can suck me off, but I don't take it up the ass. Anything else, that's extra. Cool?"

Fumbling with the dude's clothes, Richard worked discreetly to get at his wallet. The man had to have a billfold, a nice one, dressed the way he was. But he couldn't find the damn thing. It wasn't in his jacket, nor was it in his pants. That was uncool. The trick was being prissy. Frustrated, Richard gave up and said, "Fuck this shit."

He tugged at the man's sleeves and the two of them ended up sitting side by side on the pavement. Richard's nose nuzzled the trick's neck, so that when he breathed, he inhaled his hair. Cars raced in the street. Laughter from the Zuni Café disintegrated in the misty air. A Coast Guard seaplane, an ancient prop job with pontoons, sputtered over the rooftops. The flu had left Richard drowsy and weak. He nodded off with his head on the white man's shoulder and had a dream about his mother.

A mocha-skinned woman of medium height with wide-set brown eyes, she was at the corner of Ellis and Mason in the Tenderloin. She wore a straw bonnet with a blue ribbon, a yellow print sundress and leather sandals, and held an overnight bag in her hands. Her legs were unshaven and her arms were bare. An onyx bracelet glistened on her right wrist.

The sidewalks teemed with undocumented workers, fruit vendors, winos, and roving merchants selling cassette tapes in Spanish and Korean. A teal-colored Mercury sedan oozed to a stop by the curb. The driver, a middle-aged white man in a decrepit suit with no tie, poked his head out the window and asked, "You Arlene?"

She answered with a jerk of her chin. "Did the doctor send you?"

The driver's hair was slicked back with Vaseline. His face was blackened with two-day-old stubble. His skin was sallow. Worry lines were written in his mouth and there was no animation in his eyes. "Yeah, he did. Get in. We've got a long ways to go."

He opened the passenger door for her. She plunked into the front seat. "All right," he said. "You're not supposed to know where we're going. I've got to put a blindfold on you. Doctor's orders."

No one had told her about that part. No one had told her much of anything. She didn't protest—who would listen? Without a word, he tied a black silk scarf over her face. Then he disengaged the brakes and restarted the car. They drove out of the city on Highway One over the Golden Gate Bridge.

Leaving the road, they took to the surface streets of a rural town somewhere in Marin County. The Mercury's engine purred with efficiency. The sun heated up the right side of Arlene's face, which made her think they were traveling north and east. The wind was redolent of wild flowers and dried grass. Eucalyptus trees gave off their astringent scent. She smelled cows and hay in the pastures. The car bumped over holes in the road and then halted within walking distance of a white-framed farmhouse. The driver said, "We're here."

Removing the blindfold from her eyes, he helped her out of the car and directed her to a room on the ground floor in the house. She was told to wait there. Framed medical certificates hung from the peach pink walls in the room. Trays of surgical instruments sat on a chair in a corner. A sheet-covered examining table took up most of the floor.

Minutes later a tall physician in his sixties walked in the door. A stethoscope hung from his neck. A tie was loosely flung over a white medical smock. His bilious gray face was inexpressive and his movements were labored. He handed her a pink paper dressing gown and motioned for her to remove her clothes. His voice was softer than cottage cheese when he said, "Lie down on the table, please."

Undressing and then donning the gown, she did as he instructed, allowing him to insert her feet in steel stirrups. Rough and clumsy, he was unconcerned with her discomfort. He clapped on a pair of latex gloves, lubricating the fingertips with KY jelly. He asked, "How many months along are you?"

The question eliminated all the pride she had. It reminded her that she was naked in the presence of a strange man and that she was eighteen years old and on her own. Things couldn't get any more basic. There was nothing for her to give up, except what he wanted to know. "I'm three months pregnant."

His flinty eyes evinced dislike for her. When he spoke, his eyebrows went up and down, but his lips didn't move. He said, "The procedure is curettage without anesthesia. Do you understand?"

"No."

"I can't put you under because that might cause complications."
She accepted this without knowing why. "Okay."
"You have the money?" he asked.
"Yes."
"Cash?"
"Yes."
"How much?"
"One thousand."
"What size are the bills? Are they fresh and clean?"
"They're in twenties."
"Where are they?"
"In my overnight bag."
He picked up the satchel. "This?"
"Yes."
The doctor found the cash and stashed it in a cabinet. "Good, very good. Now let's begin."

Lying on the table, she hyperventilated as he went to work and scraped the walls of her uterus. She dissociated, using her mind to get out of her body. She hardly felt a thing though blood ran over the table's edge, splatting on the floor. The only sound in the room, other than the surgeon's breathing, was the neutral ticking of a clock on the wall.

She didn't remember how she got back to her parents' house in the city. By then, she was bleeding profusely. She walked in the door and said to her mother, "I've got a problem," and foundered on the living room carpet.

Streaming down her legs, blood made a puddle between her feet. Her two-year-old son bumbled into the living room, sucking his thumb. She groaned miserably, cranked her head sideways to avoid his gaze and quavered, "Richard, get the hell out, okay? Mommy's not feeling too good right now. She needs to rest. It's been a long day."

The mockingbirds in the palm trees awakened Richard Rood. The sky was buttery and low over the city. Fog blurred the streetlights.

Gunshots went off a block away. He heard a man cough and sensed something close by in the dark. He reached out with his hand to find out what it was. His fingers made contact with a regulation police department riot boot, size twelve.

A cop in a gas mask was kneeling at his side. The policeman's eyes were magnified behind the mask's lenses. He was holding a male mannequin dressed in a chic continental suit. The facsimile had a pink plastic face and a corn-yellow wig woven from synthetic fibers. Richard reflexively reached for the man he'd been sleeping with. When he found nobody at his side, he looked at the mannequin again, and drawled, "Aw, hell."

The policeman straightened up and hurled the dressmaker's model into a garbage dumpster. The dummy's legs jutted out of the bin. Getting out a pad and pen, the cop said to Richard, "Name, please."

"Richard Rood."

"Residence?"

"The Tenderloin."

"Street address?"

"Fifty-six Mason."

"House or apartment?"

"Hotel."

"Tourist or residential?"

"Residential. The Bristol."

"Telephone number?"

"I don't got one. It's been disconnected. I couldn't afford the bill."

"No cell phone?"

"Nope."

"No beeper?"

"No."

"Occupation?"

"Self-employed."

"As what?"

"Salesman."

"In what line of goods?"

"General merchandise, whatever people in the community need."

"Age?"

"Forty-eight."

"Birthplace?"

"San Francisco. I was born in General Hospital."

"Next of kin?"

"Don't have any."

"Social Security number?"

"I don't know it."

"Person to contact in case of an emergency?"

"No one."

"Now what the hell are you doing out here?"

"I was going somewhere, but I got tired and went to sleep."

"That's illegal. You can't do that in public. It's a misdemeanor. I can ticket you for it. Where were you going?"

"The Allen Hotel."

"That snake pit? You have a residence there?"

"No, I live on Mason Street."

"You got business at the Allen or what?"

"Nah."

"Who do you know that lives there?"

"A friend."

"His name?"

"Jeeter Roche."

"That dope fiend scumbag?"

"Uh huh."

"You in cahoots with him?"

"Nope."

"You selling drugs for him?"

Richard was impudent. "For that fucker? Hell, no."

"You better not be." The cop wiggled a finger at the mannequin in the dumpster. "Looks like you've got all kinds of friends." He jabbed Richard in the leg with his nightstick. "Now book on out of here before I arrest your sorry ass."

SEVENTEEN

THE HOUSES IN EUREKA VALLEY off Market Street cost a fortune, running between a half-million bucks for a one-bedroom condominium, and up to five million dollars for a two-storied house with a yard. The 130-year-old mansion on Caselli Street was an Italianate Victorian, easily worth twenty million smackers. All the windows in the place were shuttered; no cars were in the garage. A hedgerow the height of a grown man's head cordoned a sumptuous flower garden; the vast lawn was centered on a three-hundred-year-old Ponderosa pine.

Standing on his toes, Stiv sniffed the air and checked his bearings. Ninety-foot-tall redwood trees bordered the Victorian's property. Oleander bushes fronted the sidewalk. The streetlights on Caselli had burned out months ago and the road was pitch-black. Other than the moon and the fog over Kite Hill, he couldn't see anything.

Treading over a flagstone path, he walked toward the house. The garden was blooming with red, white, and pink autumnal carnations. A pensive owl hooted in the Ponderosa's upper branches. A dog with what sounded like bronchitis bayed from inside a neighbor's house.

Shuffling up a flight of marble porch steps to the front door, Stiv politely rang the doorbell. A gong chimed, reverberating beatifically throughout the Victorian. When no one answered, he tried the doorknob. Not surprisingly, it was locked. A raccoon squeezed through a hole in the oleanders and turned its manic eyes in Stiv's direction, and then did a fadeout into the garden.

Done with the front door, Stiv headed into the backyard. He lurked past a patio with a barbecue grill and an empty Olympic-size swimming pool; a cabana with a wet bar and a hexagon-shaped gazebo ran the length of the fence. A woman's drunken voice from the next street was pushed along by the wind and drifted over him.

He held his breath and pretended he was dead. It was a family trait that he'd acquired from his grandmother, a tiny Jewish woman from the Russian seaport of Odessa. She had taught him how to walk on his toes, how to open and shut windows without a sound, how to move in and out of crowded rooms without attracting an audience, and how to walk the streets without anyone seeing him.

Finding himself at the kitchen door, Stiv finagled a strip of linen cloth from his pocket and wrapped it around his hand. Clenching his fingers, he punched out the door's window. The glass tinkled to the floor—it was music to his ears. Reaching inside, he unlatched the dead bolt and darted indoors.

Trespassing was at the core of his personality. It was, as far as he could tell, fundamental to his identity. He'd been breaking and entering into houses since he was nine years old. In the beginning it had been no big thing, a small cottage here and there. Then it became an addiction. He started busting into larger houses. Nothing compared to going in an unlighted window without any regard for what was on the other side. The owner might be waiting in the dark with a gun to kill you. Or there might be a million dollars in a pillowcase under somebody's bed.

Once inside the Victorian, certain that no one had seen him, Stiv acquainted himself with the kitchen. He turned on and off the electric stove and the microwave oven, and looked in the refrigerator. There was nothing in the fridge except a gallon jar of organic mayonnaise.

He sneaked into a long hallway, and groping his way in the blackness—like a dancer with a new partner—he came upon a study with a fireplace. He bumped into an oak desk with a reading lamp. The walls were lined with books in shelves. He went to a shelf, extracted a hefty volume, and barged over to the window to read it. Moonlight underlined the hardback's cover, a book of fiction, the collected works of the Russian writer Isaac Babel. There was a photograph of the author on the back—a man in glasses with a Mona Lisa smile. Stiv had never heard of the guy and dropped the tome in a chair.

Plunging deeper into the hall, he floundered into a living room with a high-beamed ceiling. A figure-eight-shaped crystal chandelier hung from brass chains. Chairs upholstered in split-grain cowhide made a half-circle around a coffee table. A handwoven Navajo rug lay on a sofa. Carved wooden Haidu and Seneca Indian tribal masks and four large unframed abstract paintings by Gerhard Richter decorated the walls. The carpeting was plush acrylic piling. A selection of choice liquors cluttered a maple wood sideboard.

Flitting upstairs Stiv ghosted into the first bedroom on the second floor. It was an adolescent boy's room, furnished with athletic pennants and several concert posters of Van Halen featuring Sammy Hagar. There were other posters of the Scorpions, a seminal German metal band. In the comforting dark, he searched the closet. Nimble fingered, he dug into underwear, socks, photo albums and ceramic pots, stashes of cigarettes. He unearthed a vial of Oaxacan weed that he put in his jacket, and two pharmaceutical Quaaludes that he considered taking, but didn't.

The story was the same in the other bedrooms. There was nothing of value and an unpleasant feeling crept over Stiv. Ransacking bureaus and dressers, he shredded pants, socks, and sweaters with his switchblade. He went through the medicine cabinets in the bathrooms and located five ampoules of Demerol, Dilaudid and morphine, and a prescription bottle of phenobarbital, but came across no money. Irate, he broke a terra cotta lamp against the wall. What was wrong with these people?

There was a ringing in his ears; the hallucinations had left behind an auditory residue, a sign that heralded their inevitable return. Stiv redoubled his efforts in the two bedrooms on the third floor. He went to work on the beds with his blade and slashed the mattresses and pillows, hunting for secret caches. All he found was a box of Japanese porno magazines, worth no more than a hundred bucks at the flea market in Oakland. Disgusted with his luck, he kicked an antique rocking chair and was rewarded with a sprained toe. He pogoed up and down on one foot and tumbled onto a bed. He lay back, dumbfounded by the mattress's softness. There wasn't any question about it: rich folks slept better than he did.

Lacing his hands behind his head, Stiv stared at the ceiling. Market Street's far off lights did a minuet on the knotty pine–paneled walls. Through a part in the curtains, he had a glimpse of the house across the street. A simulated plaster-and-wood Tudor that had an imitation thatched roof and a Japanese maple sapling in the front yard; two BMWs and a Land Rover were in the driveway. The 1960s acid jazz of Gene Ammons was blasting from the living room.

A paunchy white male was undressing a younger woman in a second-floor dormer window. She had her hands around his bullish neck. He rubbed her heavy breasts as they kissed. His countenance was dignified. Hers was hopeful. He put his finger in her vagina, moved it, and said something in her ear. Then he pulled the woman by her wrist to a king-sized bed. The sheets were in knots, blankets on the floor. A print by the Spanish painter Goya was framed on the wall above the headboard.

Together they fell on the sheets. He got on top of her and mauled her breasts. He kneeled, his hairy ass above her, and sucked on her neck, biting and kissing the tender skin around her hairline. His hand shot out to grab a condom off the nightstand; she reached between his legs to manipulate his cock.

Tired of watching their lovemaking, Stiv uncoiled and wearily rose to his feet. His mood was bleaker than a lunarscape. Taking a matchbook from his jacket, he lit a match. It sparked in the darkness, burning down to his fingertips. In the meager light he saw his grandmother's wizened face. She was saying, I knew you'd turn out like this.

He threw the matchstick on the blankets. For a second it didn't catch, and then a flame erupted from the bed, spiraling waist-high, tinting the ceiling magenta and salmon pink. The fire, newly born and ravenous, laid into the mattress and sheets like it was starving, broiling the pillows into marshmallows. Stiv sat down on the bed and waited for the flame to reach his feet. But it moved away from him toward a wall overlooking the garden. The fire climbed onto a window; the pane was blown out in a cream of glass—Stiv flung himself to the floor as white-hot shards shrieked by his ears.

Putting his head down, he wormed his way out of the room and into the hall. Unable to see where he was because of the growing smoke, Stiv butted his nose into a cabinet. Securing the staircase, he hurdled the steps to the second floor. The fire had eaten through the floor upstairs and had burned a hole in the ceiling. Fist-sized embers were raining into the rooms below. A cinder slashed him in the face, instantly blistering his cheek. Another cinder fizzled in his quiff.

He tripped and did a belly whopper down the next flight of stairs to the ground floor. Knocking aside chairs, he vaulted through the hall into the kitchen and scrammed out the back door, swan diving onto the grass as the Victorian's roof imploded in a mushroom cap of flames.

Trampling through the garden to the street, the first thing he saw was the woman and the man that had been making love in the Tudor. They were standing naked in their driveway and gawking at the burning Victorian. The woman's breasts were mirrored orange with the fire. The man's flaccid penis was enveloped in a condom.

The second thing Stiv saw was his own right arm. The motorcycle jacket was in flames. The sleeve was roasting, the leather getting cooked from black to red. Before he could douse it, the sleeve fell off his jacket and onto the sidewalk. It lay there as if it were a carcass. Fire engine sirens jingle-jangled from over the hill. Stiv didn't see any purpose in hanging around, so he started toward Market Street.

EIGHTEEN

THE PAY TELEPHONE on the Allen's fourth floor was ringing off the hook. Five times. Ten times. Twenty times. Jeeter Roche heard it on his way downstairs. He was in his church clothes, a three-piece kelly green corduroy suit and brown wingtips. His rugged face was sweaty, his shaved scalp was pomaded; he had four ounces of uncut synthetic heroin and a copy of Somerset Maugham's *Of Human Bondage* in his jacket. Jeeter related to the protagonist in the novel, a kid with a clubfoot. He'd met several guys in prison like that—dudes that he'd celled with.

In a mad rush to meet a customer, Jeeter didn't want to tarry and answered the phone brusquely. "You have reached the Allen Hotel. If you're looking for a vacancy, we don't have any and don't expect any in the future. So don't call back, okay? You'll only be wasting your time."

The person at the other end was bossy and demanding. "I wasn't looking for a room. I've got my own place, thank you. Who is this, anyway?"

"Who am I? That's a very good question, mister. Let's start at the beginning. This is Jeeter Roche. I'm the building manager over here at the Allen, the man in charge. Who are you?"

"Jeeter?"

"Yeah, Jeeter Roche. So what can I do for you today?"

"I want to talk to someone."

"Really? This is an s r o hotel. Nine million people live here. There are a lot of folks to talk to. Now let me ask you a question."

"Go ahead."

"You calling the Allen, not many people do that. It's a rarity and I'm suspicious. Are you a telemarketer? You selling something?"

"No."

"You the cops?"

"No, I'm not the police."

"Okay. How about from the probation department?"

"No."

"You a collection agency?"

"No."

"You say you want to talk to a tenant?"

"Yes."

"Well, I don't know if I can let you. That's private information. I can't give it out."

"I'm looking for a client of mine. His name is Stiv Wilkins."

Jeeter wished a pox on Stiv and hee-hawed, "Yeah, so what about him?"

"May I speak with him?"

"That punk? What for?"

"You know him?"

"Maybe. He's overdue on the rent. That makes him my business."

"I need to talk with him."

"Why?"

"It's personal."

"Who are you?"

"Me? I'm Deflass from the mental health clinic on Shotwell Street."

"Who?"

"Deflass from the mental health—"

"I'm not deaf. I heard you the first time. I know the place."

"You do?"

Jeeter digressed. "I was there for counseling back in the day when I was on parole. Of course you understand that was before I got my shit together."

Deflass was unsympathetic and said, "Can I talk to Stiv?"

"Why?"

"We need to discuss something."

"Well, you can't."

"Why not?"

"He ain't available."

"Do you know when I can get hold of him?"

"Not really. He's being evicted."

The social worker persisted. "But I just spoke with him this afternoon."

"Is that so? Maybe you did, I can't say, but he's gone."

"Where did he go?"

"Beats me. I'm not his keeper."

"But you do know him?"

Jeeter was irritated. "Like I said, maybe."

"But you're the manager."

"So? That doesn't mean shit. It's not like he and I are friends or anything."

"You interact with him, don't you?"

"No, I don't. I just take his money."

"Then you know what room he's in. Can't you leave him a message?"

"I don't have the time."

"Please?"

There were too many people making demands on Jeeter's time. He wanted to sell the heroin, get it done with, then go home and read Somerset Maugham. A cockroach tried to sneak by him and he mashed it under his heel into the carpet. "No," he said, and hung up the phone.

126

Striped woolen drapes banked the drug room's windows. An Indian tapestry was thumbtacked to a wall next to an autographed poster from the country and folk singer Steve Earle. The rug was one of those hundred-dollar jobs from Target. Kilos of brown Mexican *mota* bulged from metal shelving. A butcher-block table was overrun with a seventy-five-pound bale of marijuana from Sonoma County. A three-paper spliff smoldered in an ashtray. A set of speakers blared King Tubby's signature dub reggae; the thud of the bass was shaking the windowpanes.

Seated on a high stool by the window, Chiclet was collating money. More accurate than an adding machine, she bagged a grand in twenties. Setting it aside, she had a toke off the spliff. She was attired in a long black skirt and a sleeveless peasant blouse, and her mouth was painted carmine red. Her hair was smothered in jasmine oil and her eyes were sprinkled with kohl powder. Gold studs were affixed to her earlobes. Her shoes were open-toed suede pumps with tassels. The cash she was counting came from the Allen's tenants. It was a collection of down-at-the-heel five- and ten-dollar bills. Rent money had less appeal than drug money. It never looked sexy. Dope money always did.

Dreamily, she looked out the window. The fog was phosphorescent in the car headlights on Market Street. She saw Mama Celeste at the corner and thought the harridan was familiar. Must be in the cleaning crew that Jeeter had temporarily hired to spiff up the building. Paid them five dollars an hour under the table. Gave them coffee and stale doughnuts for lunch.

But the longer Chiclet got a load of Mama Celeste, the more she was convinced the lady was shedding money from her army coat. Paper was falling on the sidewalk and getting blown into the gutter. Chiclet couldn't decide which one of the substances in her system was causing the mirage. It might have been the Valium. Maybe it was the Placidyl or the weed.

A tap on the door brought her to her feet. You could always judge someone by their knocking. Jeeter knocked like he was leading an army. This person sounded timid. With the elephantine spliff in hand, Chiclet bumbled over to the spy hole, fastened her eye to it, and chuckled when she recognized who it was. A miserable-looking Stiv Wilkins stood on her welcome mat. She opened the door a wee crack and asked, "What in the fuck happened to you?"

Half of Stiv's quiff had been singed to the scalp. Both of his eyebrows were gone. The blister on his cheek had ballooned into a sizeable lump. His motorcycle jacket was missing a sleeve. Shrugging his shoulders, he was in no condition to divulge his most recent misadventure. He said, "Some bad juju."

"You'd better come in before someone sees you."

It was Stiv's first time in Jeeter's sanctuary and he was impressed with the ornate atmosphere. The only lighting in the room was a brace of votive candles. Sandalwood incense was burning in a copper dish. A bouquet of roses adorned an end table. The overpowering stink of freshly harvested late summer marijuana opened Stiv's nose down to his feet.

He gumshoed it over an antique Persian carpet to the window and had a glance outside. Nighttime had turned the city into a ghost town—if it weren't for the winos, there would be nothing in the streets. Chiclet followed Stiv across the room and while puffing on the spliff, she said to him, "Listen, Stiv, we have to talk. No bullshit."

Conscious of her at his back, how close she was, he was guarded. "Please, no questions."

"Forget that. What are you doing here, anyway?"

The pinging in his ears increased its tempo. "I don't know. Maybe I don't wanna go to my room yet."

"You look totally like shit. I mean, really."

The joint she was smoking smelled tasty. It was hydroponic chronic, homegrown indica with the highest THC content known to humankind. Stiv wanted some, but it was obvious that Chiclet wasn't going to offer him any. She liked her weed too much to share it. He turned around to stare at her, but she was taller than him. It was useless trying to meet her eyes.

His motorcycle jacket looked like someone had been murdered in it. Removing it, he said, "Sorry to bug you. I'll leave in a minute."

Chiclet expelled a magnificent plume of smoke in his face. "Do you know what else?"

"What's that?"

She took her time. "You've got a problem."

Stiv scratched his head. "Who says I do?"

"Me."

"That's wonderful. What is it?"

"This guy has been looking for you."

Talking to Chiclet was like pulling teeth. You could tell she and the English language weren't on friendly terms. Not even close. And the weed had her moving so slowly, Stiv would be a hundred years old before she was done speaking. He said, "What guy? Can you get more specific?"

"Your friend."

Stiv was skeptical. "My friend?"

"Yeah, a dude came around to our house asking me about you."

"Who the heck was it? The man on the moon?"

"No, it was this dealer Jeeter knows. He was a fucking asshole."

Stiv didn't like what he was hearing. Chiclet was making a strange face. It wasn't her stoned-to-the-gills face either. The weaselly glint in her eyes was unsettling and his instincts told him bad news was in the offing. He lowered his voice to a profundo bass. "Who was it? For shit's sake, Chiclet, what are you talking about?"

"This motherfucking black dude."

He sat on the windowsill, leaving a smudge on the drapes. He didn't know what she was blathering about, and he was uninterested. He had other things on his mind and the less he knew, the better off he was. Whoever it was, it had to be someone he owed money to. Stiv was in debt to everyone. No one person in particular stood out. Debt was universal with him. He said, "You got a name for this character?"

Chiclet finished off the joint. Blue pot smoke did an arabesque in her hair. She replied, "I thought he was going to make me fuck him."

This got Stiv going. Chiclet wasn't eloquent, not even on the best of days. But neither was Stiv. Between him and her, they had the glossary of a twelve-year-old. He asked, "Who was gonna ball you?"

"That goddamn knucklehead. He had a scar on his face."

An alarm went off in Stiv's head and penetrated the jellied depths of his exhaustion. He pieced together the equation. The visitor had been black. He had a scar on his mug. He telegraphed evil. The picture grew clearer and Stiv didn't like it one bit. Uh oh, he thought to himself. The description fit Richard Rood.

Stiv's initial impression of Richard Rood had been a revelation. He had wandered into Café Flore on Market Street in June during a storm. The streets had been flooded. The sewers were backed up. He stepped into the bathroom and there was Richard humping a sixteen-year-old white boy. He had the kid up against the toilet. The lad's pants were around his ankles, his hairless legs were opaque under the bathroom's twenty-five-watt light. Richard looked at Stiv, displeased with the interruption, and then continued to toil over the kid's plum-shaped buttocks.

Stiv said to Chiclet, "Does Jeeter know anything about this?"

"He sure does. He got into a fight with the dude right in front of Martuni's Lounge. Jeeter got his ass cremated."

"He did?"

"Yeah, and that guy is looking for you like a bullet. Do you know what else?"

"What?"

"Jeeter's freaking out."

Stiv was gratified to hear this. "Why's that?"

"You haven't paid for your room this week or from last week, have you?"

He was evasive. "I'm not sure."

"Well, anyway, he's gonna evict you."

Catching her eye, Stiv was matter of fact with his answer, like he'd been rehearsing it. His wounded face was impish in the candlelight. "Yeah, sweetheart, I know that."

"You know?"

"I heard him talking about it with you on the stairs."

"You did?"

"Uh huh. This afternoon."

Chiclet hadn't offered an apology for splitting when Stiv had a seizure after going down on her. She didn't even mention it. She was more concerned about the rent. This allowed Stiv to see for himself what he was worth. He was nobody. He was a tenant who was late with his money. He was just another IOU in her ledger. The disinterested, torpid light in Chiclet's eyes confirmed it. He asked, "Do you know the time?"

"It's midnight."

He weighed her response. Every minute that slipped away was another nail in his coffin. He had to get as far away from Richard Rood as possible. God only knew what kind of state of mind the madman was in. Stiv said in a tight monotone, struggling to keep his voice level, "I gotta go see my wife and kid. We can settle the money later. Gimme an hour, all right?"

"You promise?"

Stiv threw the motorcycle jacket over his shoulders and cast a jealous eye at the marijuana on the table. He lied through his blackened teeth. "Baby, it's a done deal. You don't have to worry about a thing."

NINETEEN

IN THE HALL Stiv recognized John Coltrane's theme "A Love Supreme" pealing from a room downstairs. Hot with a fever, his lungs hurt. The metal taste in his mouth was back, and he was having difficulty breathing. "This ain't good," he sniveled. Steadying himself, he put a hand against the wall. The floor was undulating and weaving; the corridor was going round and round.

The phantom of José Reyna entered the passageway. The dead outlaw's shirt had been torn to ribbons. His chaps were covered with burrs. His holster was empty. His boots deposited a spoor of blood and dust on the floor. José was hauling a twenty-gallon glass jar with his head in it.

After driving a herd of stolen horses from Mount Diablo through the Central Valley into Southern California to San Diego County, José Reyna returned north. The police ambushed him and his band of renegades in the marshes at Diablo Creek. The temperature was 115 degrees in the shade that day. Insects weren't chittering. Birds weren't singing. The year was 1837.

José and his followers reined their horses over a precarious deer path to the creek's bottom and passed through a grove of stunted black oaks. Their pinto mounts were shaky. José was limp in his saddle, mummified from the heat.

The cops lined him up in the sights of their Sharps rifles and opened fire, raking the trees with several volleys. The sound of gunshots traveled for miles across the flat valley floor. The first to fall, José was riddled with nine bullets in his chest. Two-Fingered Tom was the next to bite the dust. Immediately their corpses began to decompose in the sun. The stink upset the cops to no end. Debating who among them was going to cut off José Reyna's head to prove they had killed the right man, they were drinking heavily to celebrate their victory. The only officer in the posse who'd been acquainted with José—the sheriff's deputy Wallace Haynes from Texas—was called upon to execute the deed.

José's body, along with the corpse of Two-Fingered Tom, was covered with leaves. José's youthful visage was peaceful, as if he were taking a snooze until the hoopla was over. Two-Fingered's countenance in death was no different than it had been when he was alive. His lips were stiff with ridicule and his obsidian eyes blazed accusingly at the drunken killers. His squirrel gun lay in the yellow sand at his feet. His straw sombrero was scored with bullet holes. Flies swarmed around the blood drying on his legs.

Four policemen with hunting knives severed Tom's hand, the one with the two fingers. The task consumed the better part of a few minutes. Then they went to work on his neck, cutting through the bone and gristle. Wallace Haynes decapitated José, hacking off the outlaw's head with a Bowie knife. When he completed the chore, he went to puke in the bushes. José Reyna's head was then dunked in a large jar filled with alcohol to preserve it. His sightless eyes stared blankly through the glass at the cops.

In later years law enforcement authorities said the head in the jar didn't belong to José Reyna. It was the head of another member of his gang. Wallace Haynes ended his life in a mental asylum in Bakersfield. Hospitalized for dipsomania forty years after the battle at Diablo Creek, the former deputy told his doctors the bandit's ghost was chasing him into the grave. Haynes passed away in the nut house, yowling that José Reyna was following him into perdition.

A year after the shootout at Diablo Creek, there was an exhibition at the Academy of Science in San Francisco. On the first day of the show, tickets were sold at a brisk clip. Since it was a weekend afternoon young parents had brought their children. Elderly pensioners were in groups of twos and threes. Out-of-town tourists fleshed out the crowd. A mustached man in bifocals and a wide-brimmed hat got in line and bought the last ticket. "It'll be a while," the usher told him. "The doors open at two."

The stranger wore a maroon corduroy suit and walked with an exaggerated stoop. His black hair was longish over his ears. He eyed the stuffed animals in the nearby corridor; lynx, tule fox, and a saber tooth tiger. When the exhibit opened at the appointed hour the ticket holders solemnly filed into the hall. "One at a time, folks, one at a time," the usher sang. "Give the person in front of you a chance to behold a premiere."

The gory spectacle confirmed what the daily tabloids in the city had been saying—it wasn't for the weakhearted. A pretty woman came away from it in tears. A child screamed for his mother. The man in the bifocals waited patiently for his turn. It wasn't every day that he spent five dollars on a ticket to a museum. Museums were dormitories for the dead; he stayed away from them as a rule. Finally the usher said to him, "Here you go, sir. You're the final person of the day. Take your time and enjoy yourself."

In the center of the room, which was painted a robin's egg white, a human head inside a glass vessel reposed on a mahogany table. The specimen's features were angular; his hair was raven black and coarse. His skin was cocoa-brown with smallpox scars. His blurry eyes had an amber luster in them. The jaded calm on his face indicated that he'd been though this before.

The usher said, referring to the jar, "Pretty cool, huh?"

Removing his glasses, the man laughed tiredly, cussing, "It's a motherfucker, all right. Thanks for letting me have a look."

The next morning the local newspaper received a letter to the editor. It said: "I went to see the exposition at the Academy of Science and I was very disappointed. The price of the ticket wasn't worth it. Despite what the newspapers are saying, that I've been captured and killed, it isn't true. That head in the jar? It wasn't mine. I still have my *cabeza* and it's attached to my shoulders. You gringos messed up. Yours truly, José Reyna."

Historians write that José fled California and returned to Mexico where he lived to a ripe old age. The headless *caballero* strode across the dingy carpet in the Allen Hotel to the emergency exit window that faced Market Street. Holding the jar that contained his skull, the outlaw lifted the windowpane and climbed onto the fire escape, leaving behind the fragrances of alcohol, horse sweat, and summer's pollen to die in the corridor.

TWENTY

THE LEGENDARY '60S SOUL SINGER Solomon Burke made a scheduled midnight appearance at Slim's, a South of Market nightclub on Eleventh Street. Champion of the ditty "Everybody Needs Somebody to Love," a pop hit made famous by the Rolling Stones, he was at present the reverend of a west side Los Angeles church.

The club was brick-walled; the audience was middle-aged and polite, black and white. The band, ten guys in tuxedos and one woman, filed out of the dressing room and mounted the stage. Rows of klieg lights, yellow and blue and red, lent a greenish hue to the sound equipment, the drum kit, the piano, a Hammond organ, a harp, and a synthesizer. A large chair with a red velvet robe placed over it was stationed behind a microphone.

The group broke into a spirited instrumental and out came Solomon Burke. He had on a bowler, fashionable Italian sunglasses, and a three-piece Edwardian suit and was enwrapped in a purple cape trimmed with ermine fur. He sat down in the chair and held out his arms to the audience and said, "Hello, San Francisco. Tonight's the night."

Evoking a spiritual, he sang in a quicksilver voice, "Raise your hands and come aboard with me." As he vocalized, he handed out roses to the women in the front. It was a mass baptism. First he'd smell the rose and then extend the flower to each ecstatic recipient as he preached. "I know there's problems out there," he trilled. "I know there are marriages that don't work and love affairs and things that go bad. But you've got to believe."

He got out of the chair, all three hundred pounds of him, tossed aside the bowler, revealing an immaculately shaved head beaded with perspiration. He ululated, "Are you with me?" A horn player came over with a towel and wiped off his pate. He invited women from the audience to climb onto the stage and dance. The band's horn section, led by the saxophonist, leaped into the crowd. Solomon Burke wailed, "This is for all the beautiful people here in the city. Don't give up, y'all. Don't give up on love."

The foggy night had folks laying low and staying at home. The gray pea soup ate at your spirit: one o'clock in the morning was no time to be outside unless you were looking for drugs or trouble.

A crew of city workers in orange vests had confiscated a homeless man's shopping cart on Market Street. The fellow, in his late forties and wearing a poncho made from a green garbage bag, was debating the workers on whether they had the constitutional right to take away his cart, which had all his stuff in it.

Richard Rood squatted in the doorway of the ACT-UP medical marijuana club and watched them argue. A leaflet stapled to a bulletin board at the club's entrance said it was customer appreciation day. All grades of weed from Mexican cartel pot to Canadian indica were discounted 20 percent off. But the black-barred doors were locked. The windows were darkened. The store's surveillance camera stared down at Richard with indifference. The place was closed until tomorrow.

His forehead itched. Of all the things he'd seen that day, the white dude Jeeter and his wife had been the most perturbing. For the life of him, Richard didn't understand how a man could have sex with a female. A woman didn't taste like a man. Didn't talk like a man. Didn't have an orgasm like one. Didn't think like one either. So where was the chemistry?

Seeing that the Allen Hotel was two blocks away, cloaked in the fog like a fairy tale castle, Richard formulated a battle plan. The question was how to confront Stiv. Being precise by habit, he mulled it over and came up with two possibilities. He could get his money from Stiv or he could humiliate him. Maybe do both. In the lacunae of Richard Rood's brain it was a matter of choices. Did he want monetary reparations from the man, or did he want to crush his ego? Either way, he was going to beat Stiv with his fists and turn the boy into mincemeat.

Before Richard Rood could finalize his plan, he heard a rustling in the bushes. Had to be a wino, or a junkie shooting up. Might be a homeless dude trying to get some rest. Maybe it was a hooker turning a trick. There were so many people living in the streets, nobody had any privacy. Folks were even camping out in garbage dumpsters.

Mandelstam was the last person Richard expected to jump out of the shrubs. The cop was overeager to get at Rood and ran smack dab into a garbage can, bruising his shins. He advanced on the black man, dragging the injured leg behind him. Richard knew he was a goner. A twenty-foot-high concrete wall was at his back. A windowless building was to his left. The cop was on his right. There was no place to go.

The policeman whomped him in the knees with the billy club and Richard, to his credit, betrayed no sign of discomfort. He masked the pain, biting his lip until it bled. Then his knee gave out and he capsized, one leg folding up under him.

Richard was seeing cops in his dreams nowadays. Yesterday he had jaywalked across Highway 101 at Vermont Street. He'd climbed a fence and had made it over to the other side and was about to hop a barrier when a Highway Patrol Jeep pulled up. A patrolman got out and demanded identification. Richard said he didn't have any. The officer stated that he was going have to take him in to the station. There was a disagreement about that procedure and the cop tried to handcuff Richard. The next thing Richard knew he was on the ground with four or five civilians sitting on top of him. He looked out from under the pile and saw that people had stopped their cars to help the officer.

He said to Mandelstam, "What the fuck do you want from me?"

Under the riot helmet the policeman's mug was tubercular white with two ruby spots on his cheeks. "That suit you have on. I hate it."

Convinced that three-quarters of the nation was against him simply because of his clothes, Richard was irked. White folks loathed a proud black man styling his threads. He complained, "It's a free country. I can wear what I damn want."

"Not if I can help it."

"C'mon, man. Lay off. It's just a suit."

"It's obscene."

"So why don't you look the other way?"

"Don't look at a man in a red suit? That's impossible, mister."

The peckerwood cop had a chip on his shoulder taller than Mount Rushmore, a fuse shorter than a pencil stub, and no brains when it came to clothing. Richard Rood sought to counsel him. "Just let it be."

"Let it be?" Mandelstam twirled the stick. "You're out here wearing that shit and you're telling me to let it be? That suit needs to go."

When a dog sees a crazy person in the street, it knows that psychosis is infectious and runs the other way to stay out of harm's reach. Human beings aren't as smart. Richard said, "Hey, wait a minute, we're talking about my vines. They haven't done a damn thing to you."

Mandelstam was inclined to differ. "The hell they haven't. They're driving me bananas. Take it off."

"Take what off?"

"Take that fucking suit off."

Richard thought it was a prank. "I beg your pardon?"

"Take the damn suit off."

"No goddamn way. Are you nuts or what?"

The sidewalk was strewn with cardboard, shopping carts, bottles and sterno cans. A medical examiner's van from the city morgue trundled up Market Street, which meant it was going to the Castro to collect a corpse. Above the cop and the drug dealer was a billboard that plugged the services of a car wash on South Van Ness Avenue.

Mandelstam unholstered his Ruger, drew a bead on Richard, and said, "Do it."

A gun pointed at your chest tests your mettle. It divides the boys from the men. It makes you understand that life is the only thing worth living for. Most people break down and cry. Some pee in their drawers. Others get their dander up and want to fight. Richard Rood was elegiac. He said, "Damn, dude, if that's what you want, what can I motherfucking say?"

Humoring the policeman, he unbuckled his pants and slipped out of his jacket, pitching the garments on the ground. All that was left on him were a pair of canary yellow cotton briefs and his Timberland boots. The underwear's waistband had lost its elasticity; the briefs sagged well below his navel. Richard's knees were shaking; the hair on his legs was sticking straight out from the evening's cold. "This is total crap," he said. "What did I ever do to you?"

Mandelstam hadn't slept in twenty-four hours and needed a shave. His riot boots had given him athlete's foot, and he couldn't find the Brinks money. He was coming down with a head cold, his second one in three weeks. He said the only thing he knew: "You were born, motherfucker."

The dealer and the cop were inches apart. Mandelstam was malodorous with apples, tobacco, and gunpowder. Richard exuded the charms of a man who hadn't bathed in a week. The gunshot scars on his abdomen were milk-white and writhed like snakes.

"Get your clothes together and get on out of here," the policeman said.

Richard Rood heeded the cue. In one motion, he fetched his suit off the concrete. Trembling in his yellow briefs, he dematerialized into the fog. He ran easterly on Market Street, hair flying, boot heels slapping against the paving stones. The Allen Hotel was one block away. Setting his eyes on the hotel's hulking shadow, Richard smiled crookedly. Things were looking better already. The sole light was in a window on the fifth floor.

That was Stiv Wilkins's crib. It was showtime.

TWENTY-ONE

THE WIND TICK-TICKED through the cracks in the room's walls. A streetlight was aglow in the window and penciled Sharona's face in shades of chrome and gold. The baby was asleep in her arms, dreaming of cats and dogs. The door opened and Stiv promenaded in with a foolhardy gait. His skin was dusky with soot. There was a hole in the crotch of his Dickies. Blood flecked his shins. The blister on his cheek had a crater with a two-inch radius.

The bleariness in his eyes reminded Sharona of the first dead animal she ever saw. It had been a blue jay in her parents' backyard. The sun had been bright and the wind was blustery. Ants were crawling over the jay. She poked at the bird with a stick, but it didn't move. That made her furious, that she couldn't get it to do anything. She said, "Stiv?"

He went stock-still at the sound of his name, like a criminal caught in the spotlight. He tried to smile, but his mouth revolted and didn't cooperate. "Yeah, tootsie," he said. "What is it? You okay?"

"Where the hell have you been?"

"Fuck, girl, I can't even begin to tell you."

She was less than enamored with his preamble. "I've been waiting all day for you."

Stiv gimped over to the mini-fridge, opened it, and looked in. The view wasn't celebratory. The bulb had burned out in a heap of green fungus and there wasn't a thing to eat, except the butt-end of a cucumber. He took a bite out of it and said, "That ain't my fault."

"I'm not saying it's your fault." Sharona kept her voice down, as to let the kid sleep. "God, you asshole, you look terrible. What happened to you?"

Stiv was noncommittal. "A little accident."

"So where were you?"

"I was at Jeeter's place."

"What did you do there?"

"I sold him a gun."

"A gun?" Sharona was incredulous. Frown lines corrugated her forehead. The seething in her eyes made her skin seem even whiter than it was. "You fuck, I thought you said were done with that."

"Well, I ain't."

"Then where did you go?"

"I went to the post office."

"What for?"

"Nothing."

"And after that?"

"I cruised over to a house I know about in the Castro."

"What's with your hair? It's horrible. You need to see a doctor."

"I ain't going to see no doctor." Stiv couldn't keep the spleen out of his voice. "Look, I've told you everything. Stop nagging me."

"I'm nagging you?"

Stiv nibbled on the cucumber. "Yeah, cool it, okay?"

That was all she needed to hear. Sharona put the baby on a blanket and rolled out of bed. Scared because there wasn't any food and terrified because she was a step away from homelessness, she mustered up what strength she had, whatever wasn't getting sapped from being with the kid, and tippy-toed over to the fridge.

Aware of a change in her demeanor, Stiv mellowed. Sharona's firm breasts were magnetized to the flannel nightgown she wore. He was hypnotized by the liquidity of her hips. He rotated to face her, and saw an apology in her eyes. He said, "What is it, sweetie, you want to say you're sorry to old Stiv?"

When her hand moved toward his face, he thought she was going to kiss him. That was nice. Affection never hurt anybody. He looked at her eyes again but couldn't interpret what was in them. She had on too much mascara to tell. Her lips were almost invisible behind a slab of sable lipstick. He closed in to smooch her, aligning his mouth to meet hers. Sharona socked him in the nose.

Reeling backwards several feet, Stiv blundered into the chair and his boots skidded out from under him. He threw his arms in the air and his chin hit the fridge door handle. Then he found himself face down on the floor. Blood trickled out of his mouth; an incisor had been chipped, and he massaged it with his tongue.

Lying there in a heap, all Stiv could see was Sharona's pedicured feet. He wanted to belt her, but he'd been there and done that, not with her, but with other women. It was in the past, and so he was righteous. She got down on the ground next to him and droned in his ear: "You're a shit."

"How's that?"

"I can smell her on you."

His pulse jumped. "Who?"

"That bitch."

Stiv winched his head and saw himself in his wife's wide-open eyeballs. He didn't look so hot. His scalp was bleeding. The hole in his cheek was infected. There was a fresh gash on his face. His hair was ruined. Sharona didn't look so good either. Her eyes brimmed with tears; her skin was blotchy and lobster-red. The black roots in her bleached hair were starting to show. Elaborating with characteristic brevity, he said, "Man, this is really fucked."

Gathering Booboo from the bed, Sharona organized a baby blanket, a milk bottle, an aspirator, a rubber ducky, a coloring book, pens, a pack of Parliament cigarettes, and a Zippo lighter. She put the brat on her back and the gear in a rucksack. Stiv touched his chin, getting blood on everything. He said, "Where do you think you're going?"

Sharona paled. She had no idea where she was heading. "Out."

"Fuck that. You can't leave."

She gave him the finger, opened the door and departed.

Stiv needed a change in scenery to digest the turn of events and he minced into the hall. Fucking Sharona. Who did she think she was? She had no right to boss him around. He might be an asshole; he wasn't going to deny it. But she didn't have to get all huffy. She didn't trust him? That was okay. But she had to have faith that things would turn out all right in the end. It was the golden rule to being cool.

The corridor was perfumed with tomato and garlic sauce simmering on a hot plate in a neighboring room, making his mouth water. Smelling the armpits of his T-shirt, Stiv decided a shower was next. There was no hot water at this hour, but he didn't care. He stank like a slaughterhouse.

The window at the end of the hallway was half-open, held up by a phone book. The sonance of cars honking and dogs barking filtered into the hotel from the street. Stiv's gaze wandered to the window and lingered there. For one unnatural moment, as if it were a chimera, he was unable to fathom what he saw. He had to be having a hallucination.

Posing in between the window's chintz curtains was Richard Rood.

The black dealer gibed, "Surprise, you bowlegged fuck."

Richard's salutation informed Stiv of three things. Richard wasn't in a forgiving mood. All the mistakes Stiv had made in the last twenty-four hours were returning to plague him. And if he didn't want to get killed, he had to leave, pronto. He shouted at Richard, "Come and get me, home slice!" and jackrabbited down the hall to the bathroom.

Your typical s r o hotel restroom is no larger than an iron maiden. It has a solo toilet, a lot of blood on the woodwork, newspapers on the floor, and no toilet paper. The house rules at the Allen Hotel stated that nobody could occupy the john for longer than ten minutes. The mandate was to dissuade the junkies in the building from shooting dope in the can.

Bolting the rickety door behind him, Stiv flumped on the baby blue toilet lid, grateful for the solitude. The commode's walls were painted vermilion. The garish color agitated Stiv, and fearing that it would trigger another episode, he shut off the light switch and sat in the dark. He crossed his legs at the ankles and fretted. He was going to die over four hundred dollars, maybe in this bathroom. The police would find him with his head in the bowl and his eyes gouged out. He could see his obituary: Stiv Wilkins, two-timing husband, father by proxy, itinerant musician.

Glancing at the tiny window above the water tank, Stiv had a brainstorm. He broad-jumped onto the toilet seat and had a chop at the pane with his hand. The glass gave way and shattered, falling five stories to the bottom of an interior airshaft. Stiv stuck his head out the jagged hole and shrewdly deduced that he could use the drainpipe to wriggle down to the next floor.

The toilet wobbled under him as he pushed off, forcing himself out the window. His girth didn't make the exit simple; he found himself jammed in the window frame and scraped his legs. Testing the drainpipe, he discovered it was sturdy enough to accommodate him. Fastening both hands on it, he shimmied twenty feet downward to the fourth floor shower room window. A rat, big as a football, popped out of a crevice in the airshaft. The rodent twitched its whiskers and bared its fangs. Stiv yodeled and flung back his head: a rectangle of fuchsia night sky was high above him.

He insinuated himself through the shower room window, descending feet-first on the tiled floor. On the way in, he lost a boot. It tumbled into the airshaft and hit the ground with a resounding plop. There were two stalls in the shower room; both pungent with Dial soap and Prell shampoo. Scum honeycombed the tiling. The floor was warped from leakage. A used condom was in one drain; a syringe was in the other one. A sopping athletic sock was exiled in the dressing area. A pair of apricot satin panties was on the shower curtain rod.

Prodding the door open with his foot, Stiv had a look into the corridor. Everyone in the building was asleep, even the cockroaches. It was deathly still, a tundra of silence. His grandmother would've loved it. He must have genetically inherited a talent for trouble from her. At age of eleven he was a regular shoplifter at the nearby Cala supermarket. No one had the brains to look at him—he was nondescript and puny. Week after week, he pilfered the store and was eating better as a result. Kids in school were coming up to him and saying, "Hey, Stiv, you're gaining weight. You're looking excellent." Then the supermarket manager, a white dude in a butcher's apron, busted him red-handed with a package of Ding Dongs. The police were summoned and Stiv was remanded into custody, the first arrest in what became an endless string of busts.

Cowering in the mildewed shower stall, Stiv experienced an overpowering gumbo of self-loathing and nostalgia. He was frightened of the things that had gone wrong and he was sad for the things that hadn't turned out right. Somewhere in between the two, he had to fight for what was sweet in his life. He dashed out of the shower room into the hall on a dead run.

TWENTY-TWO

BOOSTING HIMSELF through the window, Richard Rood scouted the hallway. Trash was all over the floor. Gang graffiti was scribbled on the walls. Cobwebs occluded the ceiling. The carpet hadn't been vacuumed in weeks. He tomcatted it up the hall and investigated the restroom. A day-old newspaper was behind the door. The sink was plugged with hair. The toilet was making water on the floor. The mirror was cracked in two. Dollops of blood speckled the toilet seat; a bloody handprint stained the wall above the window.

Richard made a study of the print. The fingers were tapered with rings on them. Stiv had small hands, like a girl. The blood on the wall had Richard mighty concerned. If Stiv was wounded, there was no saying what he would do. The boy was sensitive and unstable. He could be dangerous. He had guns and might fight to his last breath. Or he might surrender without a struggle.

A child's shrill laughter siphoned into the hall from a room behind Richard. The lubricious voice of Jeeter Roche was carried upstairs through a window connected to the airshaft. The property manager was yelling at his wife to bring him a cup of coffee in the drug room. Uneasily, Richard shifted his weight from leg to leg and plotted his next move.

Swinging out of the bathroom, he strutted toward the emergency door located at the hall's end. He pushed it open and jounced up the fire escape to the fifth floor. A hundred feet below him was the monochromatic panorama of Market Street. Crows skimmed over the trees in single-file formation. A solitary streetlight flickered on and off at the corner of Franklin. A ring of shopping carts had been bungee-corded together in the parking lot; three homeless men had a campfire going strong on the sidewalk. One of the fellows had a wire-haired terrier. The dog was chasing after a pigeon and had the bird cornered against a fence.

When he made it to the fifth floor, Richard flattened himself against a wall and got acquainted with the gloom. There wasn't enough air to breathe in the place, and what air there was stank of garbage. Just like a damn jail. There were no lights in the hall and he strained his eyes. A stark-naked junkie sallied from the bathroom; the dope fiend's eczema-blasted skin was checkered with abscesses; his dick was a squib of flesh. Getting wind of the homicidal mania on Richard Rood's face, he went back in the loo.

For the next ten minutes Richard searched the floor high and low for Stiv Wilkins. Then he came to the last door at the end of the corridor. A frayed Massive Attack concert leaflet was stapled to it. Beer cans, candle stubs, crumpled cigarette packs, Styrofoam coffee cups, and tarot cards littered the welcome mat. Richard flattened his ear to the door's paneling and listened closely. Someone was in there and it sounded like the loon was whispering to himself.

He gave the door three hard raps. As expected, there was no answer. He put his shoulder to it, testing its strength—the flimsy piece of particleboard came off the hinges and dropped to the floor with a bang. Richard stepped back, anticipating a counterattack, a barrage of bullets or a knife. But when there was no ambush, he stalked into the chamber.

His eyes roved over the room's dilapidated interior. An aluminum pot of coffee was boiling on the hot plate. Unwashed baby bottles and dishes were in the sink. A cockroach sprinted across the counter. A roll of unscented toilet paper was on the floor. Diapers were piled on the chair. The radio was replaying the six o'clock newscast about the Brinks crime.

Stiv Wilkins was hiding under the bed with a .25 caliber Beretta. Forgetting there weren't any bullets in the weapon's magazine, Stiv crawled out from under the bed's frame. His motorcycle jacket was clotted with dust balls. The ashes on his T-shirt were matted with lint. The cut on his chin had congealed into a pus-lined crust. Pistol in his fist, he faced off Richard Rood.

Stiv was missing an engineer boot and his arms were bleeding. The fire had destroyed a portion of his quiff and his Dickies were in tatters, exposing his boxer shorts and the burns on his legs. The whites of his eyes stood out in grave contrast to the soot smeared on his face. Even with his fingers on the Beretta's plastic grips, Stiv was a scaredy-cat. "What the fuck do you want?" he ranted at Richard. "I didn't invite you in here or nothing."

The room was unventilated, and Richard was appalled by it. He couldn't imagine having a wife and trying to raise a kid in the Allen Hotel. No wonder Stiv was out to lunch. Placing a hand on the chair, Richard removed a speck of dust from his cuff and hectored him. "Your daddy invited me. He said you needed a damn good whipping."

Leveling the gun at Richard, Stiv's blood pressure went through the ceiling. There was enough adrenaline in his veins to power a rocket ship to Mars. Rancor was coming off him in a hormonal mist as he bleated, "Don't you ever talk about my goddamn daddy like that!"

Richard Rood regarded the Beretta as if it were no more deadly than a water pistol. Pointed at him, the automatic was a bad joke. Something he just couldn't be bothered with. He languidly said, "You know why I'm here, you damn turkey. You owe me money."

Nearing hysteria, Stiv did his falsetto. "Me?"

"That's right."

"You think you're gonna get it?" Stiv's voice went up an octave. "This money?"

Richard contemplated the next step. The choice was his to make. Should he beat the tar out of Stiv Wilkins now or wait a little bit longer. Maybe if Stiv hadn't produced the gun, he would've been cooler. But the retard had upped the ante, and what was done was done. Lunging over the chair, he wrested the pistol from Stiv's grip.

Taken by surprise, Stiv spun on his heels and made for the window. Cramming the Beretta in his back pocket, Richard nabbed the white boy by the motorcycle jacket's collar and lifted him off his feet. Stiv battled to break free of Richard's iron grip and kicked his legs. His mealy face was brick red under the black smudges. "Hey, lemme go!" he howled. "I ain't done shit to you!"

Richard elevated the punk another few inches off the floor. Stiv was a marionette with its strings cut. His run had come to an end. He wouldn't cross the finish line in victory. There would be no applause or celebration. No accolades. Silent boos rang in his ears. Stiv had taken a gamble and lost.

"All right, you obnoxious little squirrel," Richard grated. "Where's my goddamn money? And don't even try to tell me you don't have it." He pinned Stiv to the chair and stared at him. "Four hundred fucking dollars down the tubes. Maybe I should kill you, huh? Make you die real slow."

The closest Stiv had ever come to death was during an all-night drinking bout with the Indians who consorted by the Greyhound bus station. There had been a miscommunication about who was buying the next twelve-pack of beer. A Shoshone from Wyoming had called Stiv a snake in the grass and chased after him with an axe. Stiv got away and came back with a rifle. A truce was established; apologies were made, but he stopped boozing with Indians.

Shoving him backwards, Richard catapulted Stiv onto the bed. As if he had been shot from a cannon, Stiv's head crunched into the wall. Unable to control his bladder, he peed in his boxers. Urine ran over his leg, wetting his Dickies.

Richard Rood narrowed his eyes. Stiv was flopping on the sheets no different than a fish out of water. He had soiled his jeans and was ranking up the room. There was nothing cute about him. He looked half dead with the burns on his face. Killing him wouldn't prove a damn thing. The emotion was powerful and washed over

Richard. It scared him. The futility of violence was something he'd never considered before in his forty-eight years on the planet. Head in a whirl, he didn't know what to think. Dispensing pain was his religion. Little compared to the merriment of putting the hurt on someone. But he was sick to hell of warring with his inferiors. Murdering Stiv would be a waste of calories and no more satisfying than snuffing a roach. It was better to let the bitch live and suffer. That was punishment enough. An even better policy would be to forget his ass.

Richard pulled up the chair and sat in it. He unzipped his jacket and beheld Stiv. The white boy was an amoeba under his microscope. He said, "You know what?"

Reclining on the bed, Stiv had the impression there was a lull in the action and he took the opportunity to smooth out the wet stains on his pants. He was taciturn. "What?"

"You're stupider than all get out," Richard said. "The dumbest damn thing I ever did see."

Stiv's eyes watered from the pain in his nose. "Huh?"

"You want me to repeat myself? You're stupid and ignorant."

"So?"

"Damn it, I'm trying to tell you something. Listen up because I'm having a fucking epiphany as we speak."

Stiv's curiosity was piqued. "What is it?"

"Like, fuck it."

Stiv's ears perked up. He heard an unexpected reprieve in Richard's words and it sounded promising. "Fuck it?"

"Don't you understand shit? That's what I said. I said fuck it."

"Fuck what?"

"Fuck you."

"Fuck me?"

"Yeah, you."

Stiv was let down. He was greedy and wanted more. "That's all?"

Richard ran a finger over his scar. "No."

"What else?"

"Fuck the damn money."

Stiv needed clarification. "What money?"

"You know what I'm talking about. Don't be coy with me."

"Huh?" Stiv didn't want to lose the détente that was growing between him and Richard Rood. He said, "I ain't, man."

Richard slipped him a dirty look. "You'd better not be bullshitting me. If you is, you're as good as cooked."

"No, no, I'm cool."

"Okay. You know the shit you owe me? That money?"

Stiv swallowed. He was having the worst heartburn of his life. "What about it?"

"Fuck it."

"Fuck it?"

"Yeah, what the hell. Fuck it."

"I don't believe it." Stiv was agog. Richard Rood had gone completely around the bend. The killer was losing his marbles. He said, "Holy shit. You don't want your money? Jesus . . . what for?"

Richard had come to a decision. "That's right, motherfucker. I don't want it."

"Oh, no." Stiv was flabbergasted. "Why the hell not?"

Richard Rood thought about the old lady with the shoebox and said what he had to say. "Serendipity."

Stiv had never heard of serendipity. Nobody in the streets was talking about it. None of the dealers he knew had any. You just couldn't buy it like heroin, speed, or weed. That meant one thing: it had to be an au courant designer drug that came in limited quantities with the distribution tightly controlled by the suppliers. It was something only the elite was into. Not the folks on Market Street. A pang of envy tunneled through Stiv. Richard Rood was one hip cat. He went to great parties and knew the right people. He was probably high on the shit right now.

"Hey," Stiv said. "I can get the cash for you. Just give me a little time," he pleaded. "Another day and I'll deliver it to you."

Richard wasn't having it. "Shut the fuck up."

Stiv Wilkins couldn't believe his luck. Richard Rood had abolished his debt and had spared his life in the bargain. The odds had been against it. The resurrection of Jesus Christ had been more likely. The clanging in his ears dissipated. The metal taint on his tongue went away. He lay amidst the furzy blankets flying on cloud nine. "Whatever you want, dude," he said fervently.

TWENTY-THREE

IT WAS TWO IN THE MORNING when Mama Celeste returned to the Allen Hotel. Backtracking through the foyer, she retreated up the unlighted staircase accompanied by a family of mice. A drunk in the bathroom on the second floor was softly singing "Fly Me to the Moon" by Frank Sinatra. His voice was raw, giving an edge to the upbeat lyrics.

By the fifth floor, Mama Celeste thought she was going to croak. Her throat was parched. Her feet were about to fall off. She had gas, nothing bad, but it had been known to get worse at the drop of a hat. One-hundred-dollar bills were clinging to her coat. Another one was on her baseball hat. Mama trekked down the hall to her room, unkeyed the door, gave it a nudge, and tramped inside.

Turning on the overhead light, she stripped off the army jacket, the Giants hat, and the bandanna. Then she placed the shoebox on the bed, sat down, and untied her lumpy orthopedic shoes. "Oy vey," she said. Her joints ached; sciatic pains flooded her left leg. Maybe she should take a couple of Tylenol, the extra-strength type. Tomorrow she would buy some.

The room was frigid, so she swung her legs off the ground and got under a quilt. Making herself comfy, she tallied the cash in the shoebox but quit counting after ninety-seven thousand dollars. It was nerve wracking, all the mathematics. And the gelt stowed inside the Brinks bag in her chest drawer? That was more than she dared to think about. It was enough to give her an epileptic fit. A million. Two million. Three million. Who knew? She couldn't reckon with numbers that high. They made her queasy.

What should she do with the money in the box? She needed an expert's advice. But she didn't trust a banker. She couldn't go to the cops. She didn't want to ask her neighbors. Throwing back the blankets, Mama piled out of bed and got down on her knobby knees. She put her arthritic hands together and prayed. God, she asked, what in tarnation can I do?

She waited five minutes. There was no answer. That was fine. She wasn't worried—it happened all the time. Anyway she was getting warmed up. She repeated the litany. Ten more minutes went by. She didn't hear anything. Now she was concerned. Maybe she had the wrong number. Maybe the line was busy.

Her knees ached from the hard floor, and it was cold in the room. She tried a third time. There was no reply and her spirits sank. Nobody was at home and Mama Celeste was ready to quit. Then God finally spoke. His message made her eyes bulge in their sockets; electricity crackled in her teeth. She broke into a sweat and said, amen.

Rearing to her feet, she hoisted the shoebox from the bed. She cradled it to her breasts and toddled to the window. Tying back the curtains, she inspected the city. A police helicopter ack-acked through the velour sky behind the Federal Building on Turk Street. A Muni bus with no passengers rambled by the Allen Hotel. The palm trees in the street palsied as arrows of fog blew through their fronds. A crow was on a phone booth in front of the Zuni Café. Jimmying open the window frame, Mama periscoped her head outside. The briny wind seared her skin, blowing a draft up her dress and sending a shiver down her spine. It was a sheer drop four stories to the pavement. If she fell, she'd be pizza on the sidewalk.

The cash in the shoebox shone like Christ in the manger on the day he was born. You could almost hear heavenly angels singing in the background, cherubs chorusing halleluiah. New to the world, the money was untainted by the problems that followed hard currency wherever it went. Raising the box over her head in a salute, Mama Celeste threw it out the window.

The shoebox went in one direction. The paper, one hundred thousand dollars, bolstered by the current, went flying over the street. A deluge of Ben Franklins, Ulysses Grants, and Andrew Jacksons strafed the ground. It spread out like confetti on the grimy sidewalk, inciting a riot among the five hundred pigeons that had been sleeping on the cement.

Jeeter Roche slinked out the Allen Hotel's door onto the front stoop for a cigarette. Garbed in a yellow doo-rag, a turpentine-stained tank top, and a pair of pajama bottoms, his buffed arms were sectioned with jailhouse tattoos. A collection of short stories by the Canadian writer Alice Munro was in his pajama pocket. He stabbed a tailor-made between his lips and fired it up, taking a deep drag. The bowl of opium-laced Nepalese hash that he'd smoked upstairs in the drug room was kicking in.

Despite getting his nose bloodied by Richard Rood, Jeeter was relieved with how the day had gone and surveyed the lobby with satisfaction. The rent had been collected for the landlords and was in the bank. The trash had been taken out. The floors were waxed. The walls had been scrubbed. Everything was ship-shape. When the building inspectors came next week to look at the hotel, they'd find no violations.

Things hadn't always been this good. When Jeeter came to the city five years ago, hitchhiking in from Los Angeles without a dime in his pockets, he'd lived on the street and peddled nickel bags of oregano at Hippie Hill in Golden Gate Park. The money had been bad. The police were a headache. The other dealers stole from you and smiled in your face.

The cops arrested him one afternoon and threw him in a paddy wagon with a black homeboy his age, them and a couple of Vietnam vet winos. The interior of the van had been too small for the four miscreants. The black guy wouldn't sit still; he heard somebody tampering with the van's door from the outside and threw himself at it. The door opened; the homeboy jumped out and diddy-bopped across Hippie Hill.

The park had been crowded with tourists. The police officers were chatting up three girls from Britain and didn't see him flee. Jeeter followed the black dude out and skulked past the policemen. Their mouths gaped when they saw him. The cops pursued Jeeter with their guns drawn—ducking into a grove of redwoods, he scurried through the children's playground into the bushes and lost them.

That had been the turning point in his life. Jeeter had been in and out of the state's penal system with visits to Mule Creek, Folsom, Chino, Pelican Bay, Corcoran, Susanville, and the MCC in San Diego. He didn't want to go to prison anymore. From then on he sold drugs indoors and had never regretted it.

Absolutely blinded from the hashish, Jeeter didn't notice the money that was raining down onto the sidewalks. He squashed the tailor-made under his bare foot and went back inside to go to sleep. He cut the lights in the lobby. A crow erupted from the roof's chimney and soared over Market Street in a spray of feathers. The equinox moon breached the fog and enameled the Allen Hotel in silver.

TWENTY-FOUR

THE WIND SHIFTED COURSE a few degrees and the downpouring of Jacksons and Grants and Franklins blew due east, pelting the storefronts on Market Street. The money got entangled in the telephone lines, plastered the windshields of parked cars, and fell into uncovered trash bins.

In a liquor store doorway a hundred yards from the Allen Hotel, Sharona looked at the fog as it roiled knee-high over the street. A Ben Franklin scudded, eddying, and came to rest on the baby's nose. Never having seen a hundred-dollar bill before, the infant imagined how the money would taste. Would it be sweet or sour? He snagged the note with his fingers and slurped the paper, chewing on it with a question in his inquisitive eyes. When the bill started to get yucky, Booboo regurgitated it on his mother's arm. Sharona saw what the mush on his mouth was and went, "Oh, fuck."

Cash snowed on her feet. A whirlwind of fifty-dollar bills mamboed around her head. Holding the baby in one arm, she proffered a hand in supplication and speared a twenty-dollar bill. Another Jackson was in her hair; ten more bills bejeweled her shoulders. Sharona rubbed her face in a fistful of hundreds. A trove of money blanketed the mother and child.

Richard Rood sideslipped out of the Allen Hotel and before he did anything, he scoped out the barren stretch of road from the Orbit Café to the Fox Plaza. The boulevard was quiescent; bars and restaurants were closed. The stoplights on Van Ness Avenue winked green and red chiaroscuros. The United Nations Plaza was sprinkled with the homeless and their shopping carts.

A light and harmless object brushed Richard's shoulder. It was the empty shoebox. Then he felt something else. He extended a hand to grab it and nailed a hundred-dollar bill. He brought his palms together and got a couple more Ben Franklins. Another bill hit him in the nose. He cackled in glee and turned his eyes skyward and saw Mama Celeste at her window. Bills kissed his forehead. Cash was drizzling from the heavens.

At the red light on Gough Street, Mandelstam eased on the brakes and the black-and-white slowed to a halt. The cop put his arm out the window, and as he did that, a rectangular piece of paper touched down in his hand. He squinched at it and was bewildered. He looked at the halogen-lighted sidewalks, and back at what he held. Scrutinizing the paper, he gulped hard. It had to be a vision. A perfect Ben Franklin dazzled in his palm. "Jesus Christ," he whispered. "That's a goddamn hundred-dollar bill."

Looking in the rearview mirror, Mandelstam blinked twice. Twenty-dollar bills shimmered in the road. Paper was descending on the patrol vehicle's trunk; the cash was spooky white under the moon's pumpkin orange light. Cutting the engine, he removed the Ruger from its holster. Cocking the revolver's double-action hammer, he pushed open the car door and slid out from behind the driver's wheel.

A one-dollar bill alighted on his riot helmet and lapped against his tunic. Getting into a combat stance, Mandelstam squatted behind the black-and-white's hood. An aureole of money covered the squad car's roof. The fog was cotton-dense, and he couldn't see anything. Squishing five- and ten-dollar bills under his riot boots, he stole over the sidewalk with the Ruger in his hand.

Ahead of him the snowfall of cash was blotting out the lampposts, storefronts, and pavement. The paper was beautiful, virginal and white in the street. Keeping his head low, Mandelstam plowed forward through the blizzard. Jacksons were revolving counter-clockwise in the air, getting in his eyes. Shaking bills from his uniform, he bumped into someone.

An unrepentant voice said, "What the fuck are you doing, man?"

The cop peeled a hundred from his eyes and had the fright of his life. At his feet was Richard Rood. The black dealer was sitting in a nest of money and was stuffing Grants in his jacket's pockets. His jheri curls were veiled in Franklins; his red suit was greenish-white with bills.

Under the streetlights, Market Street was a dreamland of cash. Parked cars were granulated with soggy twenties. Hundred-dollar bills draggled in palm tree fronds. Chain-link fences were tricked out with paper dollars. Richard was ecstatic and held up a wad of fifties. "See that, motherfucker?" he said. "That's what they call free money. That is jubilee. It's the closest you'll ever get to paradise."

He underhanded the fifties at the cop. Mandelstam scrunched down to pick one up. He held it to his nose and had a sniff. The cash was sweet and musty, like a wreath of flowers. It was good-looking. Usually money was downright homely. He said, "It's the Brinks dough, ain't it?"

Richard didn't respond. While the policeman sorted through the cash, the black man looked deep inside his guts and saw the writing on the wall. It wasn't a pretty vista. Jail was his next destination. The prospect made him think he was drowning in the waters of limbo. He had fifty thousand dollars in his pockets. There was another fifty grand on the ground. But what had convinced him that he could get away with the cash? He'd been no smarter than a cat chasing its own tail. He said with a drawn out sigh, "The Brinks money? Yeah, well, that shit's a hoot, huh?"

Declaring that, he kicked Mandelstam in the leg. The move bowled the policeman onto his knees. Jumping on the cop's back, Richard wrestled him to the sidewalk. Gripping the riot helmet's visor, he pulled Mandelstam's neck to an anatomically impossible angle. The lawman whipped the Ruger's stubby barrel over the black man's face, cutting open his cheekbone. Digging his heels into the ground, Richard drove a middle finger up Mandelstam's nose—the cop's septum split with an audible crack. They rolled around in the money, bloodying it. Richard slugged Mandelstam in the stomach and felt his knuckles reach the man's backbone. He brought his head up under his opponent's beefy arms and gave him a karate chop in the sternum. The police officer's heart was beating an inch away from his ears.

Mandelstam squirmed and thrust the gun's muzzle at Richard's throat. The dealer kneed the cop in the groin and the Ruger went off with a reserved bark. The shot went awry, taking one of Richard Rood's elegantly sculpted ears with it. He whooped and bit Mandelstam, sinking his molars in the policeman's nose. He didn't let go until he tasted cartilage.

The second round burrowed into Richard's forearm an inch below the elbow, breaking the ulna bone. The third shot passed through his stomach into his kidneys and drove a hole out his back, caroming off the sidewalk. The fourth round entered under his chin, making a small aperture as a hollow point bullet is designed to do. The shell went up in the roof of his mouth and into his brain. It made a flamboyant departure by taking the crown off his skull.

Richard Rood stared at the burnt sienna moon. A picture of himself as an infant zinged across the screen of his mind. He was in a frilly purple dress and white baby shoes with a yellow ribbon in his hair. His mother, splendid in a short-sleeved chartreuse turtleneck sweater, rayon slacks, and high heels, was in the kitchen cooking a pot roast for dinner. She had the radio on and it was cranking out "Bernadette" by the Four Tops. The tableau melted into the charcoal gray sky over Market Street. Sticking to Richard Rood's face was a pristine fifty-dollar bill, but he didn't see it. He was too busy crossing into the land of childhood dreams.

ABOUT THE AUTHOR

PETER PLATE, whom the *Review of Contemporary Fiction* calls "one of the most intriguing novelists writing now," is a self-taught fiction writer and former denizen of squats in the Mission District of San Francisco. His eight novels include *One Foot off the Gutter* (1995), *Snitch Factory* (1997), *Police and Thieves* (1999), and *Angels of Catastrophe* (2001), all published by Seven Stories Press. He is a contributing essayist to the *San Francisco Chronicle*. In 2004, Plate was named a Literary Laureate of San Francisco, where he lives.